"Something happened when I met you."

Eliot spoke very deliberately. At the same time he lifted his hand and touched her breast, so that Isobel gasped. "I felt as if I knew you, and you knew me. As if, between us, the ordinary processes of—courtship, for want of a better word, were superfluous. Unnecessary."

Isobel stared at him, held by the darkness of his gaze, willing her mind to blot out everything but the touch of his fingers.

"I swore to myself that I wouldn't touch you. Not unless I was sure—sure that you wanted me to."

His mouth came down hard on hers, so her lips cut off his words. "It has been so long now," he murmured incoherently against her lips. "Tell me. Tell me you want me, Isobel...."

VANESSA JAMES began a successful career in London as a critic and journalist and worked as an editor and writer for *Vogue*, *Harper's Bazaar* and the fashionable magazine *Queen*. She began writing books after her son was born, nonfiction as well as romance novels, which combine winning characters and a fast-paced style. She holds a master's degree in English and is a busy and most versatile writer.

Books by Vanessa James

HARLEQUIN PRESENTS
784—THE FIRE AND THE ICE
793—THE DEVIL'S ADVOCATE
816—THE OBJECT OF THE GAME
849—GIVE ME THIS NIGHT
915—CHANCE MEETINGS
937—PRISONER

Don't miss any of our special offers. Write to us at the following address for information on our newest releases.

Harlequin Reader Service
901 Fuhrmann Blvd., P.O. Box 1397, Buffalo, NY 14240
Canadian address: P.O. Box 603,
Fort Erie, Ont. L2A 5X3

VANESSA JAMES

try to remember

Harlequin Books

TORONTO • NEW YORK • LONDON
AMSTERDAM • PARIS • SYDNEY • HAMBURG
STOCKHOLM • ATHENS • TOKYO • MILAN

Harlequin Presents first edition March 1987
ISBN 0-373-10961-X

Original hardcover edition published in 1986
by Mills & Boon Limited

CHAPTER ONE

THE first time it happened, she was in the car; it was early evening and the light was already failing. The second time was in the supermarket, in broad daylight. The third time was at the dance. It was then she decided to speak to her stepfather about it.

The first time, Isobel was driving home and, wanting to delay the moment of her arrival, dreading her return as she always did, she took the long route back, over the Cotswold hills. The road was narrow, and she was driving slowly. She pulled up at an intersection, just as a black car sped past on the main road. She was thinking of the errands her stepfather had sent her on, checking she had forgotten nothing, for if she had, he would be in a bad temper all evening. And suddenly it happened. She saw the lights of the other car, saw it go past, saw the white signpost, the tree, the ditch on her left, and then from nowhere, her mind flooded with light. She saw nothing; no image. She remembered nothing. But she felt afraid, so afraid she began to shake. She had to stop, pull off the road, and wait, and eventually the sensation went away, and she drove home.

The second time was about a week later. She was in the supermarket, buying the week's food, for her stepfather wouldn't trust the housekeeper to do it. She was pushing the trolley along, staring at the shelves. It was a Monday; the shop was not crowded. She pushed the trolley around the food stacks, rounded a corner, and saw, at the far end, a man in a black jacket. She saw him only for a second, and only from behind. But it happened again. The flash of light, the welling up of fear.

This time it was more intense. Isobel staggered a little; she pressed her hand over her eyes, and leaned against the shelves. One of the women shoppers touched her arm kindly.

'You feeling all right, love?'

Isobel opened her eyes. The man had gone. She shook her head.

'Thank you—yes, I'm fine. I just felt a bit faint, that's all.'

The woman smiled. 'Don't blame you, love. It's that stuffy in here—like a hothouse . . .'

The third time, it was different. She had been looking forward to the dance, which was being held in a large house in a neighbouring village. Her stepfather had at first been reluctant to go, but in the end, grumbling, he had agreed, on condition they didn't stay long. Isobel so rarely went out; she hadn't been to a dance for—how long? Five years? Six? She wasn't certain. So the evening felt magical. She even danced a little herself, in spite of her stepfather's warnings. At the end of one dance the young man who was partnering her had looked down into her face. Her long dark hair was loose over her shoulders, and the young man, as if he could not help himself, had reached down and touched it. One lock had fallen forward, and he smoothed it back into place. As he did so, his fingers brushed her throat.

Isobel stared up at him. The light was blinding this time. It obliterated his face; she was conscious only of the touch of a hand. And this time she felt no fear, but an extraordinary joy, as intense, as sweeping as the light.

'Are you all right?' The young man was looking at her anxiously. It was known she had been ill, and her arrival at the party had caused a quiet but definite sensation.

'I'm fine—just a little breathless. I'll sit the next one out, perhaps.'

He took her back to her seat. Isobel sat down. She was trying to hold on to the feeling, trying to keep it with her, but she knew it had gone, and its passing left her with a sense of deep regret.

Not long after, her stepfather, whose keen eyes missed nothing, insisted they go home. Isobel went dutifully. In the car she said nothing. She sat next to her stepfather in the back, her hands clasped palely together in her lap, looking out at the winter landscape. She felt a sense of regret, and a sense of triumph.

Her stepfather had said it would never happen. But he was wrong, she knew he was wrong. Her memory was coming back. The veil was lifting.

The next day she looked at herself in the looking-glass in her room. Steadily she examined her own face. She had inherited her mother's looks—people who had known her said the resemblance was uncanny. Her hair, heavy and thick, made a halo of shadows around the pale oval of her face. Her eyes were too large for her face, she always thought. Fringed by thick dark lashes, they were a very dark blue. 'Navy-blue,' her own father used to say pragmatically. 'The colour of the sea at night,' her mother would say, more romantically.

She looked at herself levelly. The slender neck; the wide mouth; the pallor of skin. This glass was old and mottled, so her reflection was a little shadowy, like a ghost. But then she felt like a ghost. If you lost part of your past, you lost yourself, and no matter how she tried, how she searched for the girl she had been in the woman she now was, she never found her. She turned away from the glass with a sigh. That Isobel was gone. She was lost—and if it hadn't been for that light, for a sense that a shut door had suddenly opened—Isobel would have thought she was lost for ever.

She turned impatiently to the window, and looked out over the gardens. It was January, and cold, with the threat of snow in the leaden air. The gardens, so beautiful in summer, looked desolate now. Isobel sighed; sometimes this house felt like a prison. Her stepfather had moved them there after the accident. High up in the Cotswolds—a part of the country where Isobel had never lived before, where she knew no one. It was for her own sake, her stepfather explained. She

needed fresh air, quiet, rest, absence of stimulus. But
for how long? Isobel wanted to cry out to him
sometimes. It was five years now, and it felt like an
eternity.

First her own illness had been the excuse; now it was
his. She looked at her watch. Four: tea-time. The time
she went up to his rooms and, every day, took tea with
him after his afternoon rest. As always she was
reluctant to go, and as always, she felt guilty. He was
ill. She couldn't blame him for his irascibility and his
complaints—after all, the nurse said he was constantly
in pain, even with the new drugs they gave him. He had
always been good to her. He had taken her in, and
treated her exactly as he treated his own daughter
Bobby. Equally pretty dresses, equally pretty rooms,
shared treats, the same expensive schools. And after her
mother's death, when her own father had quickly made
it clear that there was absolutely no question of Isobel's
going to live with him, Edward St Aubyn had been
stern—magisterial.

'The question doesn't arise,' he had said, after
making quite sure the twelve-year-old Isobel knew
precisely what her own father had said. 'You will stay
here with Bobby and me. This is your home now. I am
your father.'

And it was true, she supposed, turning listlessly to the
door. He was. She had lived with him since she was
eight; her own father she hardly remembered and never
saw. Edward had done everything—and more. She felt
grateful, but she could not, no matter how she tried,
feel affection. And now, taking the stairs to his room,
wondering if she dared tell him about these feelings,
these sensations she had had, she wished rebelliously
that Bobby were here—that Bobby were *ever* here, come
to that; that Bobby would just occasionally take on
what Isobel acknowledged in her heart was an
increasingly heavy burden.

In her stepfather's sitting-room she paused, and her
eyes met those of his nurse in a second's mute enquiry.
The nurse, Bernice, was twenty-three, almost the same

age as Isobel. She was tough, she had a sense of humour, and she had put up with Edward's moods and rages better than any of the others. She had been here six months, and Isobel dreaded the thought of her resigning.

'Not too bad.' Bernice gave her a broad wink. 'Slept a bit better, and there's toasted crumpets for tea, so he's in quite a good temper.' She grinned. 'For once!' She hesitated then, and Isobel saw that the young nurse's face was now serious.

'The new pills seem to be coping with the pain better and the blood pressure isn't as high as it was, but ...' Again she hesitated, and Isobel saw the worry in her eyes. 'But he could go at any time. It could be very sudden. And he's still getting the pains in his chest ... I just wondered. Don't you think it might be a good idea if Miss St Aubyn came back for a while? She wasn't here at Christmas, and it's a lot for you to cope with, and ...'

'Bernice, I've tried.' Isobel felt her heart sink. She could hear the underlying message; her stepfather must not be troubled by the news of those strange flashes of perception. *I mustn't be upset like this. My heart won't stand it.* He had said that the last time she had tried to question him about the accident ... about Julius. *Why, Isobel? Why do you do it? You know what happened. It's five years ago now ... Stop fussing me, dammit. You only make things worse.*

That had been after her trip to the supermarket. She could hear Edward's voice now, angry and agitated, and knew that she dared not risk such a scene now. Swallowing her bitter disappointment, she said, 'Bobby knows what the position is. When she was here last summer I got Dr Warley to come over and explain to her. But—you know how it is. She's terribly busy, she can't give up her work. She's on a modelling session in Switzerland now. She said she might be able to come down when that was over. But then she's got to go on to New York, and ...'

Bernice's mouth tightened. She didn't like Bobby—

Isobel had seen that the moment they met—and her disapproval, if silent, was obvious. She shrugged. 'Well, I think she should be warned again, that's all. I mean, if anything happened and she wasn't here—well, she'd always blame herself, wouldn't she?'

Isobel looked away. Would she? With Bobby you could never tell. She was so wrapped up in her own affairs that Isobel doubted sometimes if the reality of her father's illness had reached Bobby at all.

'I'll try and ring her tonight, Bernice. I'll tell her.'

An hour later, Bobby arrived. She was between assignments as she always was—finished in Switzerland, off to New York, then on again to Barbados. She could stay two days, and Isobel realised that she must have worked hard to squeeze them out of her busy schedule to see her father. It seemed sometimes that Bobby never really stayed anywhere. She seemed always in motion, easily bored, only half attending to the thing in hand, as if her mind was always on the next prospect—a fee perhaps, for Bobby liked money; or a man, for she liked them too; or perhaps simply an airline timetable.

As usual, the house was turned upside down for her arrival. Mrs Spencer, the housekeeper, adored Bobby. Flowers were ordered up from the hothouses. Logs were brought in from the store. Mrs Spencer retired to the kitchen to bake. That region of the house was rich with the scents of special sauces, home-made bread, pastry and cakes—none of which Bobby would touch. Thin as a wraith, she watched her figure like a hawk; half a pound extra on the scales, and Bobby was in a black mood for the rest of the day.

She swept into the hall on a cloud of scent. Her black hair had been cut very short, her lips were shiny scarlet, and she was wrapped from head to elegant boots in furs. Isobel greeted her shyly, feeling more and more like a wraith, gauche, and insubstantial beside Bobby's vibrant colouring, her vivacity, her excitability. Suddenly the momentous news of her stirring memory appeared insignificant, not worth mentioning, and she shrank a little.

'Isobel, darling.' Bobby placed a perfunctory kiss in the air half an inch from Isobel's cheek. 'How is the old beast? Complaining as usual, no doubt? Look, I've brought him some Swiss chocolates—he's bound to love them, isn't he? He really is so frightfully greedy . . .' She broke off to survey Isobel from head to foot.

'Darling—you're looking rather marvellous, do you know that? *Much* better—there's some colour in your face now, and . . . well.' She compressed her lips, as if what she saw did not entirely please her. 'Very pretty. Frumpy old suit—why do you wear those ghastly tweeds? I'll have a talk to Daddy. You must get some new clothes . . .'

And then she was off on her grand tour, as she liked to call it. Mrs Spencer; the cleaning women; the gardeners. Bobby liked to play the *châtelaine*, and all her father's staff, bewitched by her elegance and her charm, were bowled over by it. She reappeared long enough to announce that she was going to have a drink with her father on her own, and that Isobel needn't join them—another chance missed, Isobel thought numbly—and then she was off once more. She wasn't seen again until nearly seven, when she announced that the two girls would have a late dinner together, and it would be great fun, just like old times.

At about seven-thirty she came into the library, where Isobel was reading, stalked over to the drinks table and poured herself a large whisky.

'I shouldn't do this, but what the hell.' She slammed the bottle down again with a thump. 'You want one, Isobel?'

Isobel looked up and shook her head; Bobby was clearly not in a good temper. She strode over to the sofa, and flung herself down on it decoratively.

'God! Father really can be an old swine, you know, Isobel. I don't know how you stand it . . .'

'Wasn't he feeling well?' Isobel looked at her anxiously. 'He was hoping you might come, and

sometimes, you know, excitement isn't good for him—
he can get a bit tetchy.'

'Tetchy! Is that what you call it?' Bobby lit a
cigarette, and inhaled deeply. 'And I don't know about
being pleased to see me either. Honestly—I've come all
this way. It's thrown my schedule into one helluva
mess, and he practically bites my head off! I'd forgotten
what he can be like.'

She caught Isobel's eye, and suddenly laughed.

'Don't . . .' she said warningly. 'Isobel, you've got
your preaching face on, and I'm going to stop you
before you start. You worry about him too much, you
know. In my opinion, he's as strong as a horse.
Probably see us all out. Half of it's hypochondria, and
the other half is a strong liking for getting his own way,
and generally tyrannising over people. Especially you.'
She paused. 'He did the same to your mother, if you
remember. Not mine—she had the sense to get out. But
I watched him with your mother, and Isobel—truly—he
just sort of drained the life out of her. You must have
seen that. Yet now you're letting him do the same thing
to you . . .'

Isobel sighed. 'I know all that,' she said patiently.
'And I know what happened to my mother. But . . .
well, there were reasons for that, maybe.'

Bobby took a large swig of her drink, and pulled a
face.

'Pity there weren't more. Pity she didn't go off with
her fella, if you ask me. I'm certain he wanted her to—
I remember them together—just once or twice, when we
were very little. Father was hideously jealous when he
found out. Do you—oh, sorry!'

'It's all right. And I do remember that.' Isobel smiled.
'I remember lots of things from when we were small—
it's just the later part that's blocked off. And I do
remember that man.' She paused. 'He was very tall, and
very dark, and I remember thinking him terribly
elegant. And I remember the way he looked at my
mother—and the way she looked at him. And I
remember her crying, and then we never saw him again.

I remember all that . . .' She paused. 'He was Julius's father, wasn't he?'

Bobby took a long draw on her cigarette. Her eyes met Isobel's speculatively.

'Well, well, well,' she said slowly. 'That's the first time I've ever heard you say *that* name. What's brought that on?'

'Nothing. I just wonder about him sometimes, that's all.'

'Well, don't.' Bobby stubbed out her cigarette impatiently. 'Honestly, Isobel—you've been told! All the doctors told Daddy, put it all out of your mind, that's the best thing.'

'It doesn't hurt.' Isobel raised her eyes to Bobby's. 'Look—you can see it doesn't. I can say his name quite safely. I haven't had nightmares for years. My hand is as steady as yours—steadier, come to that. Julius. There! You see? No pain. No trauma. Nothing.' Her voice was calm. She kept her eyes on Bobby's face. 'I wonder sometimes why everyone makes it such a mystery?' Now, she thought. I can tell her now, and perhaps she'll help me.

'No one makes it a mystery.' Bobby finished her drink and got up to pour herself another one. 'You've been told what happened lots of times. There had been a party, you were in his car, and he was drunk. You got thrown out, somehow, and smashed your head on a tree, and a mile down the road Julius got what comes to arrogant young men who think they can drink and drive. That's it—end of story. I thought you'd accepted all that. I can't think why you want to bring it up now, and I wish you wouldn't—I've got problems of my own without worrying about that all over again. Now listen. Have a drink and cheer up, for God's sake. After what I've just been through the last thing I want is remembrance of things past.'

She pushed a glass of whisky into Isobel's hand as she spoke, and Isobel laughed in spite of herself.

'All right, but I can't drink this stuff! I don't like the taste.'

'The taste has nothing to do with it,' Bobby said briskly. 'It's what it does to you that counts.'

She returned to her chair, and lit another cigarette. Isobel took a small swallow of the whisky. It didn't taste any better than it ever did, but she felt tired and depressed, and maybe Bobby was right—maybe it would cheer her up.

'The thing is . . .' Bobby suddenly raised her head, and looked straight at her. 'I want some money, and the old beast won't give me any.'

'Money?' Isobel stared at her blankly, and Bobby gave an impatient gesture.

'Yes, money. That stuff. Of which dear Daddy has plenty, and I—as of this moment—have none.'

'None? But I thought . . .'

'A thousand a day fees? Well, yes.' Bobby pulled a face. 'Two years ago. Not now. I'm twenty-four, Isobel. I'm getting old.'

'Oh, don't be absurd, Bobby, you're beautiful—more beautiful than ever. You never stop working. You're in demand all the time . . .'

To Isobel's horror, her cousin's beautiful face suddenly crumpled, and her eyes filled wth tears. She buried her face in her hands. Isobel rose quickly, and crossed the room, and put her arms around her. Bobby gave a convulsive sob. Before Isobel could say anything, she raised her tear-stained face. Her painted mouth was jagged with emotion, and her voice was tight.

'We've got more in common than you realise, Isobel. Much more. Your life was smashed up by some bastard of a man, and mine's been smashed up by another. And now . . .' She gave an awful, dry choking sound of misery. 'Now that old swine upstairs is going to make a third. He wouldn't give me a penny, Isobel. Not a penny. And I told him—I told him, I wished he was dead.'

She cried after that, as if she would never stop crying, and Isobel sat with her, and tried to comfort her until finally she stopped. Then she fetched her a tissue, and

Bobby blew her nose loudly. Isobel watched her closely: she knew Bobby of old. Once the storm was over, Bobby would confide. She would also feel—almost magically—a great deal better.

'Now, come on, tell me.' Isobel gave her a tight squeeze.

'You'll be shocked.'

'I shouldn't think so. Just because I get treated like a child doesn't mean I am one. Tell me, Bobby.'

'All right. It's pretty simple. And pathetic. And only too goddamned predictable! When I started out in this game . . .' She looked up at Isobel. 'It was five years ago—right? The year of your accident, as it happens. Well, it's terribly difficult to get started, and I was so stupid then—I wasn't thin enough, I didn't know how to do my face or hair or anything. I mean, I looked OK—but I didn't look good enough. Not three hundred per cent—which is what you have to look. Anyway—I went to this agency, and they were pretty half-hearted, but they gave me the name of a photographer, Liam Thomas: he's quite well known. They said he'd do some composites for me—you know, you have to have those to get any work. So I went round to his studio—and there he was. Very young and very attractive. Very persuasive . . .'

She paused. 'Oh hell—why beat about the bush? The point is, in no time at all, he talked me into taking all my clothes off, and he shot these pictures of me. Lots of them. Not very discreet pictures either. He was so persuasive—I just didn't know how to refuse . . . Anyway, I left, and I never went near him again. I heard of him, obviously, but . . . well, I almost forgot I'd ever done it. I went on a diet, had some other pictures done, the agency took me on—then there were those *Vogue* shots, you remember. And suddenly, I'm hot news. Everyone wants to use me.'

She broke off, and Isobel stared at her.

'And now he's surfaced again—with the pictures he took of you, is that it?'

'That's it.' Bobby's eyes grew hard. 'He knew the

kind of fees I was getting now—obviously he would And last month, my agent signed a new deal. A big American cosmetics company. I'd be used in all their advertisements—all their television commercials, everything. It's called product identification—I'd be the face of their cosmetics. It's worth a lot of money. It got into the papers—Liam was on the phone the next day.' She paused. 'He wants ten thousand. He says that's what he can get for them from a certain newspaper. And he knows that if they're printed I'll be finished. The cosmetics company will pull out of the deal—and all the prestige jobs—*Vogue, Harper's*—they'll drop me like a hot cake.'

Isobel pressed her hand tightly, unable to speak.

'I haven't got ten hundred pounds, never mind ten thousand.' Bobby raised her eyes to Isobel's. 'The rental on the flat's exorbitant—I'm in hock to the bank for I don't know what. I've got no assets except clothes, I haven't even got a car—I get driven everywhere. I can't get the money, I just can't! And now ... now Daddy won't give it to me. Oh Isobel, it's like a nightmare. I don't know where to turn.'

'Did you tell him what it was for?'

'Of course not, don't be a fool, how could I? I made up some sob-story, and it wasn't good enough. I tried everything. I even pointed out that most of it would come to me eventually anyway, and he might as well save on the death duties ... This house alone must be worth a quarter of a million—more!'

'I shouldn't think that went down very well,' Isobel said drily, and Bobby gave a slightly hysterical laugh.

'Too right, it didn't. He said he hadn't got any money to give, which is a patent *lie*—that he'd lost a lot on the market or some rubbish. He said I was a leech, and that I looked like a tart—and he went on and on about you.'

She looked up at Isobel, her eyes narrowing slightly. 'Honestly, Isobel, there's something a bit unhealthy about his attitude to you. He kept saying how beautiful you were and how pure you were ... well, it got on my nerves. I said—if Isobel's so pure, it's because you haven't given her a chance to be anything. else. She never goes out, she never meets anyone. She's going to end up on the shelf, and if you ask me, that's exactly where you want her ... Well, I was angry. I'd lost my temper.' She looked up at her cousin's shocked face, and grinned. 'If you ask me, I think he's going a bit gaga.'

Isobel sighed tiredly. 'He's very ill. He could have another heart attack at any moment.'

'If you say so.' Bobby leaned back in her chair. 'If he did, that would solve all my problems——' She drained the last of her drink and got to her feet. 'And don't look so shocked either, Isobel. It's what I feel, and I might as well be honest. We never got on—you know that. Because I wouldn't kow-tow to him like everyone else. And if it hadn't been for the accident, you wouldn't have either. I could see it coming ...'

'What?' Isobel looked up sharply. 'What do you mean?'

Bobby reached for the whisky bottle again. She swayed against the table as she did so. She poured out the third whisky, and then turned round slowly.

'Once upon a time you had a mind of your own. And now you don't—or if you have, you don't exercise it. He's broken you, Isobel, just the way he broke your mother, and pretty soon, if you don't do something, it's going to be too late to pick up the pieces ...'

Isobel stared at her. She felt the colour mount in her cheeks. The room suddenly felt oppressively hot.

'I had a mind of my own?' she repeated slowly. 'How do you mean?'

'What's the point in lying?' Bobby suddenly gave an angry gesture. 'You were in love with Julius Delahaye— that's what I mean. And Daddy up there was bloody furious.'

There was a long silence, Isobel stared at Bobby. Her figure became very clear and distinct, and then very shadowy. The fire flickered, and the room seemed filled with an incandescent light. It dazzled her. She pressed her hand to her eyes, and leaned back against the chair.

Bobby crossed to her quickly. As if from far away, Isobel heard the sudden anxiety in her voice.

'Isobel—Isobel—are you all right? You've gone as white as a sheet—what's wrong, for God's sake?'

'Nothing. *Nothing*. I'm all right ... Bobby.' She struggled to sit up, and grasped Bobby's hand. '*Tell* me—don't lie. I want to know, is that true?'

Bobby's face came into focus once more. She was looking guilty, and very alarmed. 'I thought you'd had one of those black-outs again. God! You gave me a scare—don't *do* that, Isobel—I thought you said you were better...'

'I *am* better—and I want to know.' Isobel turned to her fiercely. 'Now put that glass down, you've had enough whisky already, and tell me. Is that true?'

'All right, all right.' Bobby shrugged, and put the glass down. 'And don't knock the whisky either—if I hadn't had that I wouldn't have been indiscreet. Okay, okay, stop looking at me like that.' Bobby sighed. 'Yes, it's true. You were nineteen years old, a total innocent, and you picked Julius, of all people, to fall in love with. You might as well fall in love with a shark. Or a piranha. They have nicer natures.'

'I was in love with Julius?' Isobel looked at her wonderingly. 'But why did no one tell me that?'

'It was just a crush, that's all, an adolescent infatuation. You'd only just left school, you hardly knew him.' She hesitated. 'You met him, once or twice—maybe three times, no more, the summer before the accident. It was when we lived in the old house, in Devon. They still had their country place there, though naturally, after what happened between your mother and Julius's father we weren't exactly on visiting terms. In fact, as far as Daddy was concerned, they were the Capulets and we were the Montagues. Their house was off-limits. And how. But we met them—him and his brother—you remember his younger brother, Edmund? I liked him, but I was rather frightened of him. Good-looking—different from Julius, but then, no one looked like Julius.' She paused. 'Anyway, I can't remember the details. But we met up with them somewhere, and they invited us to some tennis party at their house and we went—great secrecy and daring! And that was it.' She pressed Isobel's hand gently. 'Poor you! Head over heels, which was rather a pity, because Edmund quite fancied you, I think, and he was much nicer. But you only had eyes for big brother . . .'

Isobel shut her eyes. For a second, somewhere in her mind she heard a sound; the swish of a raquet; the soft thud of a tennis ball on grass. Then it was gone. She shook her head.

'I don't remember. It's gone.' Her voice was desolate, and Bobby planted a kiss on her hair.

'Darling—don't grieve—there's nothing to remember, honestly! It was just a crush, that's all. Then Daddy found out from one of his cronies that we'd been to the tennis thing, and he went berserk. When there was no need, because nothing happened.' She lifted Isobel's face to hers, and looked down into her eyes. 'I promise you—I was there. Julius wasn't even aware of your existence.'

'Oh. I see.' Isobel turned her face away. Somewhere, somehow, she felt an obstinate sense that there was something more. Something which was getting left out . . . if only she could reach it, see it.

'And then,' Bobby's voice was brisker, 'that was that until the following winter. We went to a party at the Carnworths' house—do you remember them?'

Isobel shook her head.

'Their parents were away on some cruise or other. And we went to their bash, and so did Julius and Edmund, and somehow or other—God knows how, but everyone was pretty drunk, certainly I was—you ended up in Julius's car.' She broke off. 'You know the rest.'

'Was it a black car?' Isobel looked up at her suddenly.

'God—*I* don't know—I can't remember.' Bobby shrugged. '*Now* can I have the rest of my drink, please? And then we'd better go in to dinner—otherwise Spencer will get offended. Which is too bad, because

I'm too upset to eat anything. It's all very well, Isobel, your deciding to resurrect all this, but I've got slightly more pressing problems.'

'Bobby—I'll talk to Father for you . . .' Isobel turned to her contritely. 'Stall him for a bit, tell that photographer you'll give him an answer when you come back from New York. I'm sure I can bring your father round. If I try to do it gently, gradually . . .'

'Would you, Isobel?' Bobby swung round to her, new hope in her eyes. 'You're my last hope—and I think he might listen to you—oh, it would be such a relief! Isobel, bless you.' She placed a kiss on Isobel's cheek. Then she turned to the looking-glass that hung over the fireplace. 'My God—look at me! My mascara's all run—lend me a hanky, Isobel . . .' She dabbed at her face and patted her hair into position. Then she caught sight of Isobel's expression in the glass, and pulled a wry face. 'I know, I know! But I do feel better now—you've given me hope. And Isobel—I haven't upset you, have I? You know, coming out with all that suddenly?'

'No, why should it? It was a long time ago, as you say. What you say doesn't really alter anything. And anyway, Julius is dead.' There was a little silence. Something in her voice, perhaps a sadness she could not disguise, seemed to make Bobby uncomfortable.

'There's only one thing . . .'

'Well?'

'What did he look like, Bobby? I wish I knew.'

Bobby stared at her for an instant, her body tense, as if she had expected Isobel to ask something else. Then she gave a slightly bitter laugh.

'Darling—I told you! He didn't look *like* anything—he just looked like himself. And once you saw him you never forgot him . . .' She shrugged at her own tactlessness. 'However, if you want specifics—he was tall. And well-built, very! He had that dark auburn hair they all had except Edmund, and he had beautiful hands—he played the piano rather well. But then he could do anything. He rode superbly; I remember him on horseback. He was clever. He won some scholarship to Cambridge or something—I don't remember the details. And . . .' She sighed. 'He could be very rude—or very charming, depending on his whim. He had a temper like the devil. He used up women—well,' she indicated the handkerchief in her hand, 'let's just say fast.' She turned away irritably. 'You can't describe him. He was just—Julius. And on one point I happen to be in agreement with Daddy—the world's well rid of him, and so are you.'

Isobel felt a tiny knot of pain tighten in her temple. She looked up at Bobby. 'Did he have grey eyes?' she said.

But Bobby had turned her back on her. 'I don't remember,' she said snappishly, over her shoulder.

CHAPTER TWO

BOBBY left for New York the following morning, refusing to say goodbye to her father. Isobel had spent a sleepless night; although she had gone to bed immediately after dinner she had lain awake, sitting up stiffly in bed, staring into the shadows in the sanctuary of her room. Her mind was racing and she clasped her hands together, trying to calm herself. To have asked for a description like that ... she still couldn't quite believe she had done it. And also ... she tried to push the knowledge away from her, but it stayed obstinately in her mind.

She had lied to Bobby. She had said she didn't remember Julius, and that wasn't true. She did. She couldn't remember his face, or his voice, or the way he dressed or how tall he was—nothing like that. But she could remember his eyes. Cold, steel-grey eyes.

If she closed her own now she could see them, and she could see the hatred in them. Cold, implacable, undisguised hatred. Sometimes she saw those eyes in her dreams. She knew they were his; of that she never had a second's doubt. But she knew nothing else, and she wanted to know why he had looked at her like that, Julius who was now dead?

And why had he hated her?

The next morning she began to plan a careful campaign of appeal on Bobby's behalf. She would wait a day, until the ripples of the row might have subsided a little, and then she would approach her stepfather. It was true he was always complaining about lack of money, but, like Bobby, Isobel could not take that claim seriously. If she were gentle with him and did not antagonise him, she felt sure she could talk him round. She would first approach him, she decided, the next day.

But, as it happened, she never had the opportunity. Edward St Aubyn died in his sleep that night. A shocked and white-faced Bernice brought her the news early the next morning.

She telephoned Bobby at once in New York, and when Bobby heard the news, there was a long silence.

'I'm sorry,' she said at last, her voice tight. 'But I'm also relieved—it's no good lying. I feel—I feel *free*. And so will you, when you've had a chance to get over the shock.' She paused. 'I'm not coming back for the funeral, Isobel, I'd feel a hypocrite. Can you cope?'

Isobel said that she could; she didn't argue with Bobby, which she knew was as useless as arguing with her father had been. Opposition only made them more stubborn. Eventually she hung up. Bobby did not mention the money; she did not need to. The fact that it would now be available to her—and just as she had wished—reverberated between them, unspoken.

Isobel put on a black dress, and so did the servants. The gardeners wore black armbands. Helped by Bernice, Isobel made the necessary arrangements. Dr Warley came in to sign the death certificate, and advised Isobel to increase her dosage of the tranquillisers she was supposed to take. Isobel looked at him.

'I'm not going to do that,' she said quietly, 'in fact, I'm going to stop taking them altogether. I feel as if I don't need them any more.'

Dr Warley shook his head. Her calmness now was the result of shock, he said, and he thought she was making a serious mistake. However, he was not in a position to insist ... He left, and Isobel went to her room and threw the rest of the pills away. Then she went up to her stepfather's room to say goodbye to him for the last time.

In death Edward St Aubyn's face looked peaceful, with a calm Isobel had not seen on it for many years. She looked at him for a long time, her head bent. She thought of him as he had been in his prime, when her mother had first married him, and they had gone to live at the house in Devon. She remembered getting out of the car, holding her mother's hand, and looking up at this tall stranger. By his side a little girl in a red dress was hopping up and down impatiently. Her mother had smiled happily. 'Isobel, this is Edward, who will be your new father. And this is Bobby . . .'

Isobel sighed, and shut her eyes. Such a long time ago. Bobby loved her father in her heart, Isobel knew that, and her refusal now to come home cut Isobel to the quick. Her heart swelled with pity for her step-father; she felt compassion for his loneliness—however much it was self-caused. Gently she bent and kissed him on the forehead. Then quietly, she left the room.

Mr Shaw was the very model of a country town solicitor. Quiet, slow, conservative, discreet. When Isobel telephoned him, he expressed his condolences, the firm's condolences, and made enquiry about wreaths. He would, naturally, be attending the funeral, he said. Then he hesitated. 'Miss St Aubyn?'

'Yes?' Isobel did not correct him. It had pleased her stepfather for her to use his name, and he himself always introduced her as if she were indeed his daughter. Privately, with her friends, Isobel still used her own name of Latimer, but John Shaw was having enough difficulty getting to the point as it was.

'Miss St Aubyn. I gather that your stepsister cannot return for the funeral? She may not be back in this country for some while?'

'No, Mr Shaw.' Isobel sighed. They had already gone over this point once.

'In that case—really this is most awkward—but Miss St Aubyn, I feel you and I should have a meeting as soon as possible. After the funeral, naturally. But there is a number of important, not to say pressing, matters we ought to discuss. And I really feel they cannot be delayed . . .'

'That's all right, I understand, Mr Shaw. Would that afternoon be convenient?'

Mr Shaw agreed quickly that it would. Then he hesitated again. 'The thing is, Miss St Aubyn—well, I realise you were not cognisant of your late stepfather's business dealings—but of late, he has had—er—certain connections with a London banking house.' He paused. 'They would like a—er—representative to attend the funeral. I thought, since most of the dealings have been through me, that he might be allowed to accompany me. If you were agreeable, of course.'

'Of course.' Isobel tapped her fingers on the table before her. Goodness, he was so long-winded!

'Oh good.' Mr Shaw seemed relieved. 'The representative's name is—I have it here somewhere, ah yes . . . a Mr Richardson. Eliot Richardson.'

'Fine. Thank you, I'll make a note of that.'

'Oh—and Miss St Aubyn, before you hang up . . .' He cleared his throat. 'The thing is—I know this may seem a little irregular—but, well, when I come to see you that afternoon, when we discuss your late stepfather's will—it would be of assistance, if you have no objections—if Mr Richardson could be present.'

'I'm sorry?' Isobel stiffened. 'You want this Mr Richardson to be present *then*? But why? Surely, this is a family matter.'

John Shaw sighed. 'Miss St Aubyn, I'm afraid I rather have to insist. You will understand fully in due course. Meanwhile, I can only say that Mr Richardson's presence would be of great assistance. Great assistance.'

'Very well. Shall we say three o'clock, then?'

Isobel hung up quickly, pressing her hand to her eyes. The most terrible blinding ache had started up in her head, shooting like a current from temple to temple. She gasped, and leaned against the table. Something was wrong—terribly wrong, she could sense it from John Shaw's polite evasions, from his obvious embarrassment. But it was not that which made the pain arc through her head. It was the name. Richardson—Eliot Richardson.

She opened her eyes, the room blurred. Desperately she searched her mind—but no, she could think of no one she knew called Richardson, certainly no one with the Christian name Eliot. And yet . . . and yet. She drew

in her breath. The pain was already ebbing. And yet—
when the solicitor had first mentioned that name she
knew it meant something to her—knew it had some
association. It had happened again. He had said the
name and she had felt an instant of blinding happiness,
fierce light. And then, yet again, the door in her mind
had swung shut.

She gave a little cry of despair and frustration. What
was *wrong* with her. Was she ill? Was she never to
remember?

The fifth time was at the funeral. She came into the
church with Dr Warley. It was raining, and overcast
outside; inside the small village church the light was
poor. She began to walk slowly up the aisle, past the
rest of the meagre congregation. It was very cold and
her steps sounded immensely loud on the stone floor;
her breath misted the air. She brushed past black-
coated figures, looking neither to right nor left.

And then it happened again, this time more
violently than ever before. Blinding light. She staggered, and Dr Warley caught her. She saw the anxiety
in his eyes, then she shook her head. The light had
gone. She walked on.

Now, back at the house, she sat before a huge log fire
in the drawing-room, as the clock ticked nearer to
three, and she grew tenser and tenser. Mr Shaw had not
returned to the house after the funeral. She had
glimpsed neither him nor the mysterious Mr Richardson
at the graveside; they must have left immediately after
the service.

Nervously she got up and stood before the fire, trying
to compose herself. She heard footsteps; the door
opened. Isobel stared across the room, frozen. John
Shaw had come in first; he was advancing now, looking
embarrassed, saying something. But Isobel did not see
him, or hear what he said. Transfixed, she stared at the
man who had quietly followed him into the room, and
who now stood near the door, looking at her.

He was very tall, and wearing black. An immaculately-cut black suit; white shirt, black tie. His hair was black; conservatively cut, it fell forward slightly over his dark straight brows. He was staggeringly, electrically handsome; the planes of his face slightly harsh, the mouth dour and unsmiling. Although he neither moved nor spoke, he at once dominated the room effortlessly, eclipsing the solicitor. Quite simply, he held the eye; and he radiated threat.

Isobel stared at him, frowning slightly. She felt every instinct in her body and mind electric with knowledge; she responded to his presence as an animal responds— not rationally, but through the sharper, quicker knowledge of the senses. Immediately she knew, just knew, that beautiful though he was, silent though he was, she did not like him, and she did not trust him. She feared him. Slowly, reluctantly, she looked at his eyes. Their gaze was hard, and utterly cold. They did not shift from her face.

Mr Shaw's greetings tailed away into an embarrassed silence. He looked at his companion, then at Isobel, with an expression of bewilderment. 'Miss St Aubyn— this is Mr Richardson, of whom we spoke on the telephone. Mr Richardson, Miss St Aubyn.'

'Of course.' With difficulty, Isobel forced herself to smile, to step forward. She held out her hand.

For one terrible moment Isobel thought he was going to ignore her hand. Then he, too, stepped forward. His fingers closed over hers tightly, then were quickly withdrawn.

'Miss St Aubyn.' He inclined his head slightly. 'My condolences.'

He had a low, clipped voice, without a shred of sympathy in it. He made the formal response without any effort whatsoever to inject sincerity into it—as if he had utter contempt for such procedures, even while he observed them. And utter contempt for her too, Isobel thought confusedly. She met his eyes once more, and then looked away, feeling a great tide of relief sweep up through her body. His eyes were brown! Thank God, they were brown. Just for a moment, when he had first come in, she had thought, she had expected, that they would be grey.

And that was stupid. The possessor of those grey eyes was dead; long dead. She would never see them again—except in her dreams.

'Please sit down.' Nervously she indicated the chairs before the fire. She sat down to the right of it herself; John Shaw sat down fussily on the sofa to her left. Eliot Richardson took his time. She saw his eyes take in the room with one casual glance. The paintings, some of them by her mother; the old and valuable furniture. Then he sat down opposite her, and his gaze returned to her face.

'Well, now ...' John Shaw cleared his throat. He opened a briefcase and took out some sheaves of paper. He looked exceedingly ill at ease, Isobel thought, as if unsure to whom he should defer—herself or the hard-faced Mr Richardson, whose elegance and self-possession made John Shaw look like a country bumpkin.

'Well, now. The thing is, Mr Richardson, as I have explained, although Mr St Aubyn's death was sudden, he had been ill for some time. And so, in addition to the unhappy circumstances of the recent days, Miss St Aubyn has been under a great deal of strain for many months. As I think I mentioned, she herself has been ill, and so I should like, if we could, to proceed gently in this matter, which is of some complexity—especially for a young woman with no experience of business affairs.' He smiled uneasily, and made a courtly gesture in Isobel's direction.

'As you see fit.' Eliot Richardson gave him a cold glance. 'What you have to say seems remarkably simple to me. A child could grasp it. I'm sure Miss St Aubyn—whatever her inexperience—will find no difficulty in the matter.'

He looked across at Isobel as he said this, inflecting the word 'inexperience' in a way that seemed to her very odd. She felt her colour heighten. John Shaw moved his papers from one knee to the other, looking more and more uncomfortable each minute.

'Well, then, before I read you your late stepfather's will, Miss St Aubyn, I should just like to explain certain things. Since the sale of his interest in his family's engineering company, as you may or may not know, your stepfather lived on the interest on his capital and on his various investments. Some of these were—well, I'm afraid I have to say that they were incautious. To such an extent that some three years ago, Mr St Aubyn found himself in a condition of some financial embarrassment, and was compelled to take out various loans—arranged by Mr Richardson here, through the auspices of his banking corporation. Unfortunately . . .'

He hesitated, and glanced from Isobel to Eliot Richardson, who was regarding him with undisguised impatience.

'Unfortunately, Mr St Aubyn's financial position worsened over the last few years. Interest rates are high, as you know perhaps, and loans cannot be obtained without security. Most of Mr St Aubyn's assets had been—er—disposed of at an earlier date, and so . . .'

'Look,' Eliot Richardson's voice cut in coldly, 'I think it would be better if you came to the point, Mr Shaw. At present you are wasting my time, which is valuable, and you are also wasting Miss St Aubyn's.' He stood up, and looked down at Isobel. 'I regret, Miss St Aubyn, the position is perfectly clear. Your stepfather died without assets. This house, and everything in it, belongs to me.'

There was a dead silence. John Shaw blushed crimson. Isobel stared at the man who looked down at her so coldly, who had spoken without a shred of tact or sympathy, and felt the blood drain from her face.

'To you? Everything?' Her eyes widened. Her first thought, winging into her head, was Bobby. Hesitantly she stood up. 'You mean . . . you mean, there's no money? Nothing?'

Eliot Richardson's lip curled, and Isobel knew at once what he was thinking. He was thinking that she was a mercenary, hard-hearted woman: every line in his face revealed that. She swung round to John Shaw pleadingly.

'But it's not possible! I never dreamt! I thought . . .'

'Miss St Aubyn, believe me. I am most terribly sorry . . . There was nothing whatever I could do. Naturally, I proffered advice, on numerous occasions. If your stepfather could have been persuaded to sell this house some years ago, or to . . . to curtail his style of living, this might have been avoided. But he refused to do that, and . . .'

'But Bobby!' Isobel interrupted him passionately. 'He can't have left Bobby nothing! She was his own daughter. She thought—she expected—she was depending on . . .'

'As were you, also, no doubt.' Eliot Richardson cut in in a sarcastic voice.

'Mr Richardson, that was uncalled for . . .' For the first time, Mr Shaw showed signs of anger. 'This is a most unhappy situation, as I thought you understood. You gave me your assurance, that, in the circumstances . . .'

'So I did. But then you gave me to understand that Miss St Aubyn was physically frail, and bereft with grief. I see no evidence of either.' His eyes flicked up coldly over Isobel's face and figure. 'Indeed, she shows a far greater ability to get to the nub of the matter than you do. So perhaps I might answer her question.' His eyes met Isobel's. 'Mr St Aubyn had no money and no assets to leave, either to his daughter or to you. He has, indeed, left nothing. There are some further debts, of course, which may not be realised by the sale of this house and its contents, and I shall have to consult with my directors as to whether they feel they wish to press for their payment.'

'Sale? You're proposing to sell this house—and everything in it?' Isobel stared at him, her voice choked in her throat.

'But certainly.' He looked at his watch, and stood up.

'But it was my stepfather's *home*—he loved this house!'

'I'm afraid that's irrelevant.' He snapped his answer irritably, as if she too were wasting his time. Isobel stepped back from him; her eyes were blurring with tears.

'I don't understand. It's not possible ... I can't believe it ...'

Dimly, through her tears, she saw his face. He was standing with his back to the light, and as she stepped back and looked at him, the light grew brighter and brighter. It was obliterating him, the room, her mind, everything. It was white-hot; she felt it burn her face.

She knew she was going to faint. She reached one arm out wildly for the chair behind her, and she felt herself start to fall. She fell slowly, as if from a great height, and from nowhere a black-jacketed arm reached out, and caught her.

'He's gone back to London.'

'What? You let him go—just like that?' On the Transatlantic line, Bobby's voice echoed with disbelief. 'You idiot! You fool!'

'Bobby—please try to understand. I ... I fainted. It was such a terrible shock. And he was so horrible—so cold. So totally without sympathy. By the time I came round he'd left—and then I talked to John Shaw. He went over the figures with me, Bobby, and it's all true. There's not a penny. In fact the estate is still in Richardson's company's debt ...'

Bobby swore. 'You're so bloody feeble, Isobel. Fainting like that—if only I'd been there! I'd have done something. I'd have got round him somehow—you always can, there's always a way.'

'You *should* have been here,' Isobel said quietly.

'Don't start on all that. I couldn't be, and I can't be now—especially now. If this is true then I've got to work—harder than ever. I'll have to try and get that money somehow—I staved Liam Thomas off, Isobel, stalled him. He said he'd wait until I got back from Barbados in two weeks' time, but that's it. If I can't get the money to him then ... Listen!' Her voice rose

suddenly. 'What about a loan? After all, if they lent
Daddy all that money, surely they could lend us a bit—
what's ten thousand to some plutocratic bank—it's
peanuts!'

'Bobby, you need security for a loan,' Isobel said
patiently. 'We haven't *got* any security. He owns the
house and everything in it. Why would anyone lend us
money?'

'Don't be so defeatist, Isobel. You can *ask*, can't
you? The worst he can do is say no, and he might say
yes. Use your imagination, for God's sake—tell him
we're destitute . . .'

'He's not going to believe you're destitute!'

'All right, all right. Tell him *you* are. After all, it's the
truth. What are you going to do? Where are you going
to live?'

'I've thought of that. I'll have to find a job, obviously.' Tiredly, Isobel pressed her hand against her brow.

'Then tell him you need just a little capital, a small
loan, just to get started. That you'll pay him back—
with interest!' Bobby's voice grew more excited. 'That
would be OK. Then you could give me the money, and
I'd let you have it back in instalments. Once I'm doing
that cosmetics job, I'll *have* the money—don't you see,
Isobel? It'll work, I'm sure of it. The man isn't a
monster, he must be human. Go to him, and open your
eyes wide, and plead—it always worked with Daddy,
why shouldn't it work with this Richardson man?'

Bobby's voice had taken on a sharp edge, and it hurt
Isobel. She wanted to protest, but she bit the words
back. When had she ever pleaded, she wanted to say,
except on Bobby's behalf? 'I'll try. But I don't think it
will work.'

'Make it work,' Bobby cut in. 'Ring me the moment
you've seen him—promise?'

'All right.'

'Angel . . .'

Bobby hung up, and Isobel replaced the receiver. She
felt exhausted. The thought of seeing that man again
filled her with greater despair than anything. If only she

felt stronger physically, then, she thought, with a spark of anger, then she knew she could have stood up to him, and answered him blow for blow. But she did not feel strong. She felt ill; her head ached, and she had no appetite, no energy; she could not sleep. Bernice, seeing her white face that morning, had been impatient, and definite.

'Look,' she said, taking Isobel's arm. 'When are you going to admit it to yourself? You're not well. Go on like this, and you'll have a breakdown—and who's that going to help? If you take my advice, you'll see a specialist. Tell Dr Warley you want a second opinion. Warley's all very well; he's kind, he's well-intentioned, but he's getting old and he paid a great deal too much heed to your stepfather in my opinion. You ought to see someone better qualified—someone who can look at your whole case history with fresh eyes. Promise me you will, Isobel—I'm worried about you. The headaches have come back, haven't they?'

Isobel nodded and grasped Bernice's arm. 'Oh, Bernice. Do you think there's something physically wrong? Is that what you're saying?' Hideous images swam up in her mind, and Bernice frowned.

'Look, I can't say. But you had a head injury—you know that. Probably it's just the strain of all this, but you should check, Isobel. Get a thorough examination . . .'

She had done as Bernice said, because although she didn't want to admit it to anyone else, she was secretly alarmed. What she had taken to be symptoms of her memory returning—might they not be symptoms of something else? So she had telephoned Dr Warley, and he was making an appointment for her to see a diagnostician in London. He had seemed relieved—and that too had worried her. Three bad phone calls, she thought ruefully. One to Warley, one to Bobby, and now, the worst of all, to Eliot Richardson. She picked up the small pasteboard card he had left behind him. It bore his name, an address in the City, and a telephone number.

There was no point in putting it off, she thought dully as she reached again for the telephone. She would have to do it, and the sooner the better. She dialled the number. It took a battle with three secretaries before he finally condescended to come on the line—but Isobel was glad of it. The arguments angered her; she felt her own vitality seep back a little.

'Miss St Aubyn?' His voice was cool and clipped. She felt sure he was looking at his watch.

'Mr Richardson.' She made her own voice equally cool. 'We need to meet, and we need to talk.'

'I do so agree,' he said, taking the wind totally out of her sails. 'Can you come to London? Perhaps you'd have dinner with me?'

Not a restaurant; not a club; his apartment.

Isobel bent her head against the wind and the rain, her sense of anger and resentment increasing. She knew just why he had insisted on that, she thought. He didn't want to be on neutral ground; he wanted to be on his territory. It could only strengthen a position that didn't need strengthening.

And where did he live? Why, in a part of London she didn't know, of course. A part which had grown up and expanded and flourished in the years she had been closeted away in the country. In the Barbican, at the top of one of the towers in the penthouse suite. 'Take the express elevator,' he had said, crisply. 'It only comes to my floor.'

She looked around her at a concrete wilderness; the tall buildings created a wind tunnel. The wind tore her hair; the rain lashed her skin. You might as well be out on Dartmoor, she thought, thinking of the countryside, bleak, beautiful, threatening, which had surrounded her in her childhood. And she felt, just for an instant, a tug, a pull, there and then gone, as if memory had been plucked, just for an instant. She stopped, and looked up at the immense building before her. This was it; too tall to see its summit through the rain; a pillar of lights. She imagined he would like that, that it would appeal to

him, to live so high up, with London a tiny place spread
out before him. *And he saw the countries of the world
spread out before him on either hand...*

She smiled wryly to herself. And which was Mr
Richardson? Satan or Saviour?

The security man was eventually persuaded to let her
in. The elevator accelerated so that her heart lurched
and her ears hummed; the doors hissed back. And there
he was, waiting for her, unsmiling, wearing a black
dinner jacket, narrow black trousers that emphasised
his height. He did not hold out his hand, he hardly
troubled to greet her. He merely held back the door to
his apartment.

She went into an enormous room, head held high,
and for a moment her eyes dazzled. There were huge
windows, uncurtained, looking out over a city of
shadows and lights; the city did not look small from
here, she realised with a gasp, nor insignificant. It
looked breathtakingly beautiful: a magic city that she
felt she could almost reach out and touch.

'May I take your coat?'

He reached up. His hands brushed her neck. Isobel
froze, gripping her nails tight in her palms as the feeling
flooded up through her, fierce, strong—like fire in the
blood. He was looking at her with polite curiosity.

'Are you all right? You're not about to faint ...
again?'

'I don't make a practice of it.' She snapped her
answer, and shrugged off her coat. Without waiting to
be asked, she walked into the room, and sat down. She
looked around her. The room must have been forty feet
long at least, and equally wide. The ceiling was very
high, and at the far end stairs led up to another space,
open to this one, where she could see a table laid for
dinner. Everything in the room was beautiful and
modern: she looked around it curiously. The carpet was
cream, the furniture was white; there was a Corbusier
chair, a Mies van der Rohe sofa—collectors' pieces all
of them. Paintings were abstract. It was a beautiful,
costly, cold room After the jumble of old furniture and

possessions in her own home, it was doubly startling.
Instinctively she turned to the fire; it blazed brightly,
contained in a hole in one wall by a perfectly geometric
frame of polished steel.

'What would you like to drink? I have most things
. . .' He paused. 'Whisky? Vodka? White wine? Why not
have a glass of champagne? You look cold.'

'Thank you.' She nodded abstractedly, her eyes
returning to the room. It was curious, for she hardly
knew him, yet she would have said they were not at
one. The man, for all his icy formality, and the icily
elegant surroundings were somehow at odds with one
another . . . She took the long flute of cold champagne,
carefully avoiding contact with his hand. He stood
looking down at her, at the full black velvet skirt of her
dress that belled out over the white cover of the chair.
Isobel looked up at him.

'What a beautiful apartment you have.' She
hesitated. 'Forgive me if I seemed to be staring at it. It's
something of a shock—after my stepfather's house. It's
so modern, you see, and I'm used . . .'

'Yes. I prefer not to live in the past,' he said crisply.
'Literally and metaphorically.'

She looked up at him curiously, struck by something
in his tone. 'Do you find that easy? Most people might
not.'

'I'm practised at it.' For the first time since she had
met him, he smiled. A cold smile, that lifted his lips and
did not reach his eyes. 'Sometimes it's very easy. At
other times . . .' He looked at her and then abruptly sat
down. 'At other times not.'

Isobel gave a wan smile. 'That makes us opposites.
You want to forget the past, and I want to remember
it.' She broke off, wishing she hadn't said that, for she
had no desire to discuss her illness with him. He leaned
back in his chair.

'Ah yes—John Shaw mentioned something about
that. A car accident? Some form of amnesia, I think he
said?' He smiled coldly. 'I've always found that
particular condition rather difficult to credit.'

Isobel flushed at his rudeness. 'I might have said the same once. I wouldn't now.'

'Really? How fascinating. Do tell me—how does your particular form of amnesia work? Can you remember nothing before a certain date, or only certain things? Are the shutters permanently closed, or do they occasionally open? Does a veil obscure things, and then, occasionally and obligingly lift? That's the appropriate cliché, I think, veils, shutters, doors—is it not?'

Isobel put down her glass and stood up. 'How can you speak like that?' she said hotly. 'How can you? If I said I were blind or deaf, would you take the same attitude? Why are you so unbearably rude?'

'I apologise.' There was nothing apologetic or conciliatory in his tone. 'You are, as you say, afflicted. You have my sympathy. Indeed, I often wish I were similarly afflicted myself. However ...' He leaned forward quickly. 'Please stay where you are. Don't leave. After all, we have business to discuss.'

Slowly Isobel sat down again. She did so reluctantly. Just then she wanted nothing so much as to walk out, never to have to speak to this overbearing, insolent, insufferable man. But she thought of Bobby, and what Bobby had said, and so she obeyed him. She took a sip of champagne to give herself courage, and then turned back to him. To her surprise he was looking at her now with some amusement; mockery flickered in his dark eyes, as if he found her not only contemptible, but also fake. She said in a low voice:

'I'll come straight to the point. I know your time is valuable, and I don't want to waste it. After you left my stepfather's house ...'

'*My* house,' he corrected smoothly. Isobel's eyes flashed at him, but she refused to be drawn.

'After you left, I went over my stepfather's will, and over the accounts with Mr Shaw. I see quite clearly that everything you said at that meeting was true.' She paused. 'My stepsister and I are left with nothing, we both understand that. I spoke to her on the telephone— she is working in New York, and I explained the

position. However . . .' She hesitated. 'Plead', Bobby
had said. But how could she plead to this man? Her
spirit rebelled at the thought.

'It's very difficult for me,' she went on. 'Bobby is
working but because of my illness, and then my
stepfather's heart attack, I haven't worked for some
years. It will take time for me to get a job, and find
somewhere to live, and . . . and it would help me greatly
if I had just a little money behind me.' She drew in her
breath. 'And so—so I wanted to ask you if your
company would consider giving me a loan.'

'I see.' His eyebrows rose. Slowly he picked up a pen
from the table beside him, and unscrewed its cap. He
produced a small memo pad and a calculator from an
inside pocket. 'How much had you in mind?'

'Ten thousand pounds.' Isobel had to force the words
out. He raised his face and met her eyes.

'Ten thousand? I see. On what repayment terms?'

'I thought—I thought you might tell me that.'

He gave a small, cold businesslike smile. 'We could
discuss that. But a fairly normal arrangement for a sum
of that kind—given your circumstances, and trying to
be of assistance—let me see.' He punched the keys of
the calculator. 'Charging you at our normal rate of
interest, say 14.5 per cent, the APR is slightly higher of
course—I'm just giving rough figures now. Monthly
repayments of the order of £300, spread over—shall we
say a three-year period? Yes, I think I might be able to
arrange that.'

'You could?' Isobel felt her heart lift. Three hundred
a month sounded horrendous to her, but no doubt to
Bobby it would seem feasible.

'Oh yes. On what security would that be?' He put the
question lazily, almost off-handedly, but Isobel was not
deceived. She stared at him.

'I have no security—you know that.'

'Oh dear.' He flicked the notebook shut; recapped the
pen. 'Then I'm afraid, of course, that we can't be any
help.'

'But you *knew* that.' Isobel stammered. 'You know I

have nothing I can put up as security. But when I have found a job—when I have a salary—I thought then—on the strength of my prospects.'

'Miss St Aubyn, will you forgive me if I tell you quite frankly that from a business point of view your prospects are very poor? You haven't worked for five years. You have been ill, I imagine you are untrained. It's quite likely you would not get a job at all—and frankly, if you did, I think it unlikely it would pay enough to enable you to meet our requirements. I'm afraid the answer is no.'

'I'm not asking for charity, damn it!' Isobel sprang angrily to her feet. 'I'm asking you to lend me money, at a high rate of interest, which I would repay! Not everyone would dismiss my prospects, as you call them, quite so out of hand! I can work! I had a good education—I'm not a fool and an idiot even if you treat me like one . . .'

'Do sit down.' He lifted his hand. 'I had no intention of insulting you, I'm just explaining to you the realities of the situation . . . you have to live in the real world now, you know.'

There was a silence.

'What do you mean by that?' Isobel said at last. 'I can understand reality as well as you can.'

'Of course.' He stood up smoothly. 'Shall we have dinner now? We seem to have started off on the wrong foot. Why don't we just sit down, and you can tell me a little bit more about yourself, and your plans—and then I can advise you.' He paused. Very deliberately, his eyes fell from her face to her body, and then back to her face. 'Maybe . . . maybe there's another solution we can find to this problem.'

He doesn't mean what I think he means: he can't! Isobel stared up at him. He was looking at her now in a way that terrified her, and which he did not seek to disguise. It was the swift cursory sexual appraisal of an experienced man. Her breasts, her legs, the curve of her hips; her loose hair: all this he took in at a glance, unemotionally, as if he were sizing up a car, or a racehorse he was about to purchase. No one had ever looked at her in that way before; she tried desperately to convince herself that she was wrong now. He smiled.

'Did I say how very beautiful you were looking?' he said. 'Black becomes you. Now—shall we go and eat?'

CHAPTER THREE

THE table was glass; the cutlery was Jensen silver of geometric design. The food—which was delicious—had been prepared, and left, he said carelessly, by some 'girl' who cooked executive luncheons at his bank.

'I, however, chose, the Burgundy,' he said, as they moved on from delicate artichokes and prawns, to the main course, which was pheasant. He lifted the bottle. 'It's the 1980. It should be rather good . . .'

Isobel looked up at him quickly, but said nothing. 1980: the year of her accident. And that reminded her of something else. Just now, she was sure of it, he had said she had been ill for five years. Now how had he known that? She was almost certain she had mentioned no date. She looked at him, but there was nothing to suggest the choice of year for the wine was deliberate—perhaps John Shaw had told him, she thought. That was probably it.

'It's a little young—it could wait. But still . . .' He tasted it and then looked up at her. 'It was a good year—for Burgundy.'

They ate for a while, and as they did so, and as she drank some of the wine, Isobel felt herself relax a little. Once they had sat down at the table, his manner had unfrozen slightly. She felt almost certain that she must have interpreted his attitude earlier quite wrongly. Now his manner was quite ordinary, and almost kind: it was that of an older man patiently drawing out a somewhat tongue-tied young woman. She glanced up at him, trying to estimate his age. Early thirties? Mid-thirties? It was difficult to say.

'Now.' He looked up at her. 'Supposing you tell me a little about yourself?'

'There's not a great deal to tell.'

'Well, tell me about your family.' He smiled, as if

41

trying to encourage her. 'During our business involvement, you see, your stepfather and I never met ...'

'Really?' Isobel looked up at him in surprise. 'Isn't that rather unusual?'

'No, it was a fairly routine matter. A small affair as far as we were concerned.' His eyes looked away. 'It was arranged mostly through intermediaries. I didn't know, for instance, that he was so ill. So—tell me. Had you always lived with him?'

Isobel sighed. 'My own father is alive,' she began. 'His name is Latimer, Philip Latimer. Usually I preferred to use his name—but it upset my stepfather, so at home I was called St Aubyn. It was easier.' She shrugged. 'It avoided rows.'

'I see.' He laid down his knife and fork. 'And do you often see your own father?'

'Never. He's a sculptor. He's lived in Cornwall for years. He and my mother split up when I was very young, four or five. I hardly remember him. Then, when I was eight, my mother married Edward St Aubyn—he was divorced too, and he had a daughter almost my age—Bobby. She's a model, the one who's in America now.'

'Ah yes, that's right. John Shaw told me about all that.' The question of Bobby did not seem to interest him greatly. 'And he said your mother was a painter—yes?'

'Yes, she was. You probably didn't notice, but there were several of her paintings in the drawing-room when you came to the house,' she answered carefully.

'A painter? Interesting. Married first to a sculptor and then to a businessman. And was her second marriage a happy one?'

The question took Isobel by surprise. She lowered her eyes.

'I don't know. Possibly not—I think they didn't have a great deal in common. But my stepfather was always very kind and generous. And my mother died when I was twelve——'

'And you remained with your stepfather,' he finished.

'But not at the present house, I think John Shaw said . . .'

'No, we lived in Devon then. Near Dartmoor—my stepfather's business interests were all in the West Country, and he liked it there. So did I.'

'I know it well.' He smiled. 'I have a house there myself, as it happens—not that I have time to visit very often. I inherited it from an uncle a few years ago . . .' He raised his eyes to hers. 'It's in the hills to the west of Totnes. You know Totnes?'

'Oh, of course.' Isobel smiled. 'It's so lovely there . . .' She broke off. 'Yes. I miss it sometimes.' She paused. 'I haven't been back there, you see. We moved—my stepfather decided to move—after the accident.'

'Really?' His eyebrows lifted slightly. 'And why was that?'

'Well—it was for my sake really. I had been—quite ill. And the doctors told him that a change of scenery would help. Quiet. Rest. New surroundings. My stepfather had retired, so we moved.' She looked at the watchful face across the table. 'It was very generous of him—I mean, I realise you probably don't have a very high opinion of him, for letting his business affairs get into such a mess, but he was a very kind man. I'm sure he can't have wanted to leave Devon. It was all done for my sake.'

'The accident must have been a bad one.' He cut across her remarks. 'Does it upset you to talk about it?'

'No.' Isobel took another swallow of wine. She felt much more relaxed; and it was such a relief to talk and not to be told not to rake up the past. 'But then I can't really talk about it, I don't remember it at all.' She hesitated. 'I was nineteen. It was the year after I'd left school. Bobby and I went to some house—it was a typical teenage party, I suppose. The parents of the girl who gave it were away—there was a lot to drink. Someone gave me a lift home, and there was a crash. That's all.'

'And you don't remember any of that?'

Isobel shook her head. 'Nothing. It's as if . . .' She

hesitated, and raised her eyes to his face. But he did not look bored, or irritated, he was looking at her with a cool dispassionate interest which somehow made it easier to talk. 'It's as if I had lost two years from my life,' she said in a rush. 'The year before the accident, and the year after. I ... I was in a coma for some months, you see, and then ... My next memories are very fractured. Of the hospital, a little. And then my stepfather, and then going to the new house in the Cotswolds.'

'Quite extraordinary.' One finger tapped on the glass tabletop. His eyes did not leave her face. 'I've read of such cases, obviously ...' He paused. 'And what happened to the driver?'

'The driver?'

'The person who gave you a lift.'

Isobel felt the colour mount in her cheeks. She looked quickly away. 'He was killed. I was thrown out of the car, and he crashed into something further down the road. I don't remember him at all.'

'How tragic.' His voice was flat. There was a little silence. 'Did he have a family?' He paused. 'Parents? A wife?'

Isobel looked up at him startled.

'Oh no—he wasn't married. And his parents were dead, I think. He had a brother—but we, I, hardly knew them. I never saw any of them again. My stepfather wouldn't have allowed it. He blamed him, you see.'

'As you must do, presumably?' He put the question coldly.

Isobel shook her head. 'No—I don't,' she said slowly. 'These things happen—we were all very young. And besides, in the end, I was all right. I recovered. He died.' She felt suddenly cold. 'Please—let's not talk about it any more. It's not really relevant, is it?'

'I thought you said you didn't mind talking about it—that it didn't affect you?'

'Well, it does.' She turned her head. 'If I think of him it does. It makes me—sad.'

The word was inadequate. She knew it, and he certainly seemed to think so, for with an abrupt gesture he tossed his napkin on to the table, and stood up. He suggested brusquely that they should sit by the fire again, and that they should have some coffee.

He took some time with coffee and with brandy before he returned to her, and his manner was abstracted and thoughtful, as if he were working something out in his own mind. When he returned, he sat down next to her.

Isobel folded her hands on her lap, half-regretting what she had said. She wished now that she hadn't taken this man into her confidence; she felt a little cheapened for doing so. It was not his business, not his affair.

'Please,' she began, her voice more brisk, 'I don't want you to think I came here tonight to tell you a sob-story. I didn't. I probably shouldn't have started on all that . . .' She gave a wry smile. 'I expect it was the Burgundy loosening my tongue. But I'm quite well now, I intend to get a job. And you said you would give me some advice in spite of my poor prospects.' He gave her no answering smile.

'Ten thousand,' he said meditatively. 'How did you arrive at that particular figure, I wonder?'

'Well—I . . . I worked it out.' Isobel flushed. She lied badly, and she was aware of it. 'I thought I would come to London and take a secretarial course. I'd have to pay for that, I'd have to find somewhere to live. The course would take a minimum of six months—I checked. And then I might not get a job immediately, as you said. It seemed—a sensible figure.'

'I see.' He placed the tips of his fingers together, and regarded her thoughtfully. Isobel was intensely conscious of his proximity, of his watchfulness, and it made her very nervous.

'I suppose I could go somewhere else, to a local bank, something like that. If I hadn't needed money quite so much, I would never have . . .'

'I said your business prospects were poor,' he

interrupted her. 'I didn't mention other kinds of prospects.' He turned to her as he spoke, and his level dark gaze met hers. Isobel stared at him.

'Other prospects?' she stammered.

'It would be difficult for me to help you professionally—through my company. But I might be able to help you personally.'

'You could?' She stared at him, mesmerised, held by the hardness in his eyes.

'I'm not poor.' He gestured around the room and shrugged. 'Ten thousand seems a modest request. I could accommodate that very easily, in certain circumstances.'

'I don't understand.' Isobel turned her face away. She felt alarm, but she also felt a sick welling-up of disappointment. When they had spoken at dinner, she had found herself beginning to like him, almost to trust him. She couldn't believe he was about to suggest what she read in his eyes.

'Look at me.'

His voice was suddenly sharp. Isobel turned her face to his unwillingly. He was looking at her closely, his eyes shadowed, a slight twist to his mouth, as if he were trying to read her face.

'You know,' he said slowly, 'you have very beautiful eyes? Extraordinary eyes. I've never seen any quite like them. But there's something in those eyes—I don't quite know what it is. An evasion. Something . . .' He paused. 'They look as if you were dreaming. *Her eyes are open, but their sense is shut* . . .' He quoted the line lightly, but she saw his brow contract in a frown, his mouth tighten. 'I think it would be very pleasurable, and very interesting to wake you up. Worth a great deal . . .' He leaned forward. 'Don't you?'

Gently, and before Isobel could move, so hypnotised was she by his low voice, he raised his hand to her throat. He stroked the soft skin there, slowly, his eyes never leaving hers. Isobel stared back at him, her eyes widening, a pulse beginning to hammer in her temple. He was regarding her questioningly, searchingly, as if her face could tell him something. When she did not move, or draw back, he sighed. Then, slowly, deliberately, he lowered his mouth to hers.

His lips were firm against hers, and warm. As they touched hers, Isobel felt light explode in her mind and her blood. Instantly, as if he had thrown some switch, she felt a surge of response, so strong and so unexpected that she gave a low moan.

At once, with a peculiar desperation, his kiss deepened. His arms tightened around her, he drew her against his body passionately, with a kind of desperate longing and protectiveness, as if tenderness and want fought for domination. Almost at once, his control seemed to snap; he kissed her with a terrible, pent-up longing, impatiently, as if willing her response, as if he had been starved of a woman's body and a woman's mouth. Isobel's lips parted beneath the soft pressure of his tongue, and he groaned against her mouth. Fire shot through her blood; before she could stop herself she felt her hand tremble then relax against the sudden hammering of his heart. Her mouth felt full, swollen by his kissing; she shuddered, and felt his hand, pressed against her spine, tense, hesitate and then, as if he could not stop himself, slip round caressingly over her rib-cage and up to the swell of her breast.

His fingers moved gently, delicately, over the thrust of her nipple against the black velvet, and at once she felt a startling sharp pleasure, as the full aureole hardened under his hand. He cupped her breast then, in his palm, through the soft material, and then moved it away, his kiss growing gentler, until he held her again, cradled against him. His lips moved on hers, lightly; then he drew back.

They stared at each other. Isobel was trembling. His face was grave, she saw, troubled, and curiously stern. He hesitated, as if about to say one thing, and then deciding against it. Isobel's mind swirled with light and darkness, with a drowsy hypnotic pleasure and an odd sharp edge of fear. He looked at her almost sadly, she thought, trying to force her mind to function normally; and with a regret that made no sense.

'Now,' he said at last, his voice low. 'Tell me you were lying.'

'Lying?' Isobel stared at him. The question took her completely by surprise, and made no sense to her. For one wild moment she thought she must have misheard—then, with a leap of comprehension, she realised. The money: of course, he meant the money. He knew she had been lying about that.

Colour washed up over her face and neck. She drew back from him, turning her face away miserably. She knew she must look guilty, and she felt his hand tighten for an instant around her waist. Then he released her.

'You *were* lying.' His voice had taken on a sullen desperation. 'I know you were. Haven't you the grace to admit it—now?'

'Now?' Isobel swung round to him indignantly. 'Now you've kissed me—is that what you mean?'

'Yes—now I've kissed you. Absolutely.'

His voice was so bitter then, and suddenly so cold, that Isobel felt pain dart between her temples. Shakily, she pressed her hand to her forehead. The room was utterly still; the man beside her didn't move, though she could feel that his eyes never left her. At last, with a sudden quick angry gesture, he rose to his feet and turned away from her.

'Forget it. I must have been mistaken. I shouldn't have done that.' His voice was filled with a cold finality edged with distaste.

Slowly Isobel raised her face to his, bewilderment and unease swirling in her mind. His mouth had set in a harsh line.

'Why did you do it?' She forced the question out, and his eyes flashed.

His voice was heavy with sarcasm. 'I took you for a different woman. Didn't you realise that?'

She felt a knife of pain, a tightening of the muscles in her throat. She had to make herself speak at all, and

when she did, the calm of her own voice surprised her.
'What do you mean by that?'

'You want me to spell it out? All right.' He
shrugged once more. 'I kissed you because I wanted
to—I would have thought that much was obvious.
And . . .'

Isobel turned her face away. 'I see what you must
have thought. I should have stopped you at once.'

'Then why in hell didn't you?'

She drew in her breath shakily, feeling anger start to
rise in her blood. 'Because that has never happened to
me before. I . . . I didn't know what to do, and . . .'

'You knew exactly what to do. Don't lie! And don't
try and tell me you're inexperienced either.' His voice
rose in sudden anger, and he broke off. He paused,
hesitated.

'You knew what I wanted,' he went on, an odd
uncertainty in his voice. 'You must have done. And
besides—you wanted it too.'

'That's not true!' Isobel's eyes flashed and she rose
indignantly to her feet. 'I wasn't prepared. You took me
by surprise, and besides . . .' Her voice shook. 'As you
say, you took me for the wrong woman. You didn't kiss
me because you wanted to—you kissed me because you
were making a bargain. If I agreed, if I didn't resist—
then you would lend me the money I need. That was it,
wasn't it?'

She paused, but he made no answer. Isobel lifted her
chin. Well, maybe he didn't want to admit now the
sordidness of his bargain, but she knew she was right.
The hell with him!

She pressed her hands together, and went on, hearing
the tension in her own voice. 'Perhaps *I'd* better spell it
out. No—I'm not the kind of woman who'll go to bed
with you for ten thousand. Or ten million, come to that.
And now I'd better go.'

'Then do it because you want to.' His words stopped
her in her tracks. 'Because I want you to.' His mouth
curved in a bitter smile. 'I never mentioned any such
bargain. . . . Come to bed with me for the sake of it.

The money can be thrown in for good measure, or not, as you like. I couldn't care less.'

'Well, I could!' Isobel stepped back from him angrily as he lifted a hand towards her. 'And don't touch me! You—you disgust me!'

'I shouldn't have said so.' A muscle contracted in his cheek, and she saw his eyes darken with a sudden anger. 'Quite the reverse. A moment ago, in the heat of the moment, as it were . . .'

Isobel's fingers itched to slap his face, but she restrained herself, held, in spite of her indignation, by something in his voice.

'I'd have said,' he went on slowly, 'that you were responding to me. Is that so difficult to admit? For a woman who appears so—maidenly—' His mouth twisted with irony. 'I'd have said your response was— quick. I found that exciting—perhaps I went too far. But the excitement in my case is only just abating. It could be rekindled very swiftly if you were prepared to admit what you felt. And then—well.' He smiled. 'We could have a very pleasurable—and interesting— evening, don't you think? So, why not stop edging towards the door, and stay. Come to bed with me.'

Isobel gave a low cry of anger, and his mouth tightened.

'Maybe the change of ambience would upset you? In that case, let's stay here and make love on the sofa. Anywhere you like . . .'

'Make love? Make love?' Isobel rounded on him furiously. 'That's not the term I would use in these circumstances!'

'I'll use another then, if you'd prefer greater directness.' He cut across her words, and stepped towards her, smiling rather tautly. 'Miss St Aubyn— why don't you come here and let me . . .'

Isobel hit him. She brought her palm back, and smacked him across the face with the flat of her palm as hard as she could. Then she stepped back, shaking. Slowly he raised his hand to his cheek; there was a red weal against the pale tan of his skin, the imprint of her fingers.

He gazed at her, his eyes darkening, the corners of his mouth twisting in an ironic smile. 'Who would have thought it? Such a little she-cat . . .'

He turned away from her to the fire, and Isobel, shaking, her mind pulsing with anger and shame and indecision, stared at his averted back for what seemed like an eternity. She knew she ought to leave, or apologise—for whatever he might have said he had shown her no violence, and she had the impression that his words had been goaded out of him—there had been self-hatred in his face as he had spoken them. But she could bring herself neither to speak nor to move, and eventually it was he who turned and spoke.

'Do you know,' he said slowly, 'that's only the second time in my life that a woman has hit me? And the first time the consequences were very serious.' He paused. 'I'd like to tell you about them.'

Isobel opened her mouth to protest, to interrupt, to say something, anything, that would stop him short and get her out of the room. But no words came. In spite of herself she was held, as mesmerised by his manner now as she had been when he kissed her. His face was grave, his voice quite steady, but the emotion he felt was clearly strong: she could feel it, an unseen force, eddying across the room to her.

'That first time ... there were repercussions. Considerable ones. And as result of them I stood trial.'

'*What?*' Isobel's eyes widened.

'The intial charge was rape.' Slowly he raised his eyes to hers. 'It was untrue, and mercifully it was dropped. The woman in question wouldn't testify on that charge.'

Isobel swallowed. He had paused, his eyes searching her face, as if he expected some response from her—fear, perhaps, she thought. She hesitated, then spread her hands with a little hopeless gesture.

'Why are you telling me this?'

'You've told me about yourself. Why shouldn't I repay the compliment?' He smiled, but there was no amusement in his eyes, only a bleakness. 'I can tell you the final result, if you like. I can tell you the sentence. I

did two years—reduced to just over one for good
behaviour.'

'You've been in prison? You? I . . . I can't believe it.'
She gestured at him, at the room. He gave a short bitter
laugh.

'You mean I don't look like an ex-con? That ex-cons
don't live like this? Well, you're right, I suppose—in
most cases. I was fortunate. I had friends who stood by
me, and I had money. That helps.'

'What was the charge?' Isobel leaned forward,
impulsively, still hardly able to believe what he said.

'Oh—didn't I say?' He smiled, his eyes glittering
darkly against the pallor of his skin. 'It was one of the
more poetic in the judiciary system. Also one of the
oldest. It was Grievous Bodily Harm.'

Across the room their eyes met. Isobel hesitated:
there was something very odd in his manner. He spoke
as if he were throwing out a challenge, tossing some
gauntlet at her feet. She frowned.

'Are you telling me the truth?'

'Oh yes.'

'But *why* are you telling me? I hardly know you,
and . . .'

'I want you to know.' He cut her off suddenly, and
took a step towards her. 'I want you to know—who I
am. What I am.'

'Then tell me one more thing.'

'Yes?'

'Tell me—were you guilty as charged?'

'I was judged guilty.'

'But you were innocent!' She sprang to her feet
impulsively, her eyes searching his face. 'You didn't do
it! You can't have done! That's what you meant
earlier—when you said you wanted to forget the past—
you wanted to forget that—because you were punished
for something you didn't do? Is that it?'

To her consternation and bewilderment, she realised
there was now a plea in her voice.

'You seem to have a touching faith in me suddenly. I
hate to disappoint you, but really, the answer to your

question isn't as straightforward as you think.' He turned away, his voice flat. 'Moralists would have us believe that the desire to commit a crime makes a man as culpable as the crime itself. And if that's the case, then, yes, I was culpable. I was guilty as charged. I wanted to kill her,' he said softly and deliberately. 'But then—I loved her very much.'

To her own astonishment, Isobel felt a sudden insane spurt of jealousy for this unknown woman. He looked at her face, his brow contracting for a second, as if her expression puzzled him. Then he shrugged.

'Desired her. Wanted her. An all too predictable and familiar obsession of the flesh. Literature is full of such cases, and I ... well, I am not as cold as I perhaps seem.' He turned away for a second, his voice flat and without energy. She saw him hesitate and knew he already regretted whatever impulse it was that had brought on this extraordinary confession.

'You want to leave. You wanted to go some while ago. I'll fetch your coat.'

He disappeared into another room without further words, and Isobel stared after him. She could not analyse what she felt, she was incapable of analysis. All she knew, with every instinct in her body, was that she believed him to be innocent, in spite of what he said.

And he had told her—why? Because he wanted her to know the worst about him, she thought, because he expected her to be shocked, horrified, to rush out and avoid seeing him again. It was as if, quite deliberately, he had made himself vulnerable to her ... She pressed her hand, tremblingly, against the hammering in her head. Everything seemed to be accelerating at enormous speed, as if she were on some train she could not get off, and it was rushing her on, into the dark.

She felt no fear, no hesitation, no rationality at all. She just wanted to stay on that train, ride that speed, let it carry her into the dark. She let her hand fall. Would she have felt like this, she thought, if he had not kissed her?

He came back, and put the coat around her shoulders. His hand brushed against her neck.

'I want to see you again.'

He made the statement flatly, and without either emotion or hope, as if he were stating the dullest of facts, and expected an indignant refusal.

'I want to see *you* again.' The words sped to her lips before she had time to think.

His eyes met hers, and she saw something light in them, quite suddenly, altering the aspect of his whole face. He smiled.

'How honest you are. Sometimes.'

He opened the door, and pressed the button for the lift.

'When do you go home?'

'Tomorrow.' Isobel looked away. She had to see the specialist in the morning. 'Tomorrow afternoon.'

'I'll drive you. I have business with John Shaw anyway.'

The lift had arrived, and he held the doors open. She turned to go, her heart beating wildly and fast; then, on impulse, remembering his earlier words, she turned back to him.

'The money,' she said hesitantly. 'Please—I'd like that never to be mentioned again. I'll . . . I'll sort it out. I'd just prefer it if—if you could forget I'd ever mentioned it.'

'I'll try.' His voice was suddenly clear. Isobel stepped into the lift. 'But I don't have your ability to forget things, unfortunately.'

Mr Stevenson's rooms in Harley Street were on the first floor of a large and opulent house. It had a wide and handsome staircase with steps of polished marble, and a thick carpet of dark blue wool. Halfway down that staircase, out of sight, she hoped, of Mr Stevenson's receptionist above, and the waiting-room receptionist below, Isobel stopped. Above her the door closed behind the next patient; below her a clock ticked.

With a ragged sigh, her breath choking in her throat,

she let her body sag back against the wall. She didn't want anyone to come; she couldn't bear to be seen, not just now. Somehow she had managed to get through the rest: Mr Stevenson's slow patient examination; the gentle and persistent questioning; the final part of the interview: *Miss St Aubyn, I think there is something you ought to know* ... She had got through all that: she thought he had no idea of the shock she felt. She'd left the room, nodded to the receptionist, passed the next patient on the stairs—all that, the matter of a few minutes, and they had seemed to her like hours.

It was ironic, really. When he said that, her heart had almost stopped beating. She'd thought he was going to tell her she was seriously ill, that there was some lasting damage as a result of the accident, clinical damage, that explained the loss of memory, the new symptoms over which he had so closely cross-questioned her. And she had been quite wrong. She saw now, the point of all the earlier questions—what he had been leading up to.

Miss St Aubyn, apart from reducing your intake in tranquillisers, has your life altered in any way recently— altered emotionally, I mean?

She hadn't understood him, even then. At first she thought he meant her stepfather's death, then, illogically, her mind had winged back to the night before, to the scene with Eliot Richardson—and then she had understood. He meant, was she in love? Did she have a lover? Had she ...

And then it had gone on, wave after wave of inconclusive detail which told her everything and told her nothing. Even to remember it now, and the shock of hearing it—these, the most intimate, the most personal details of her life, being spelled out by a stranger—even now the blood swept up her throat and flamed in her cheeks.

He had not understood, she thought miserably. He told her something that shattered her whole conception of herself one moment, and talked cheerfully and encouragingly about 'normal teenage behaviour' the next. He had patted her hand in an avuncular fashion, and told her there was no reason for shame or embarrassment, that it was better she knew and came to terms with the knowledge, and she had sat there, docile as a child saying nothing, and wanting to scream aloud. She didn't feel the way he said she ought to feel—calm, believing everything would sort itself out in due course. She felt none of those things. Instead she felt a terrible fierce anger: anger that she had been lied to, however well-meaningly. Anger that still, even now, nothing came back.

I want to know, she thought. I want to know! It's not fair—it's cruel—how can I forget something like that— the time when my whole life must have changed . . .

She drew in her breath to steady herself. Very deliberately she forced herself to walk down the remaining stairs and out of the door.

Who? she thought. Who had possessed her, and been forgotten by her?

Was it Julius? Was that why she dreamed of his eyes— was that why he had hated her?

CHAPTER FOUR

ELIOT RICHARDSON picked her up at her hotel. He was driving a large black BMW motor car: a conservative car—a banker's car, she thought. He drove across London, and up on to the M40 flyover, fast, and impatiently, saying little, keeping his eyes on the traffic. His silence suited Isobel; she stared out of the window at the passing streets. London seemed grey, dismal and interminable, and her mind felt like that too, a place of brick walls and culs-de-sac. Rain lashed the windscreen; after a while he glanced at her, and then silently slipped a tape into the car stereo. Music flooded the car, a Mozart opera. It soothed her, and lifted her spirits a little.

'You're very quiet,' he said at last, as the tape came to an end, and she opened her eyes and found they had left London behind.

'I'm sorry, I'm just a little tired. Where are we?'

'Approaching Oxford. We could stop somewhere the other side and have lunch. Go for a walk if you like— the weather's clearing—have you eaten?'

'No, I haven't.' She hesitated. 'But—I know you have business to attend to. I don't want to delay you.'

'If I thought that I wouldn't suggest it.' He smiled. 'We'll stop just beyond Burford. There's a place I know there.'

He pulled in finally to a courtyard in front of a beautiful old pub. It had a garden, with a stream. One swan was poised on it, watching them. Eliot smiled. 'It wants sandwiches, poor thing. In the summer all the visitors feed it, and in the winter everyone's inside. Will sandwiches be all right, by the way? It's late, getting on for closing time, and alas, we're in England. There certainly won't be anything else.'

Isobel forced a smile. 'Sandwiches would be

lovely—I'm not that hungry. And I'll save a bit for him.'

The pub was almost empty. A couple of people who were clearly regulars were sitting at the bar, talking to the landlord. Eliot found them a niche at the back of the room that overlooked the gardens. It was snug after the cold of the air outside; across the room a log fire flickered.

'What would you like to drink?'

'Oh, a glass of wine. Thank you.'

He disappeared back to the bar. She could hear his voice ordering the drinks and the sandwiches. She looked out across the damp lawns; there, behind the house, the stream widened. The swan—was it the same one?—was moving back and forth on the water. As she looked, it bent its head to reach for some piece of weed, and then lifted it again. Water ran in a cascade over the long arch of its neck, over its back between the curve of its wings. Isobel looked at it, and she started to cry. The tears came silently, welling up from her eyes, falling down her cheeks, and on to the table. She looked at them and knew it was ridiculous, and knew she couldn't stop.

She felt an arm come round her, and she tensed, bending her head, so her hair fell forward to hide her face. He said nothing; he just kept his arm around her shoulders, and at length, as the tears grew fewer, an immaculately laundered white linen handkerchief appeared in front of her. She dried her eyes, and got her breath. Deeply embarrassed, she looked up.

'Now—eat this, and drink some wine.' He sounded surprisingly kind. 'Then, when you're feeling better, tell me why you're crying. I don't usually have such a disastrous effect when I take people for lunch.'

'It's not you—I'm sorry.' She shook her head, and handed him back his handkerchief. 'That was totally stupid. All it's done is make your handkerchief all wet.' She took a sip of the wine, and a bite of the sandwich he offered her.

'I don't agree at all. Tears are a release—the worst

thing anyone can do is hold them back. I often think
the world would be a great deal better a place if there
were no convention against men crying. Which doesn't
mean I'm going to weep just now—but if you want to
again, don't worry in the least. I shan't mind.'

Isobel smiled wanly. She finished the sandwich, and
drank a little more wine. Then she leaned back in her
seat and pushed her thick hair impatiently back from
her face. 'There—I'm better. It was nothing.'

'Why did you cry?' He was looking at her levelly, and
he put the question gently.

'I was looking at the swan, it looked so beautiful.
And then I started to cry. No proper reason.'

'You're very tired.' Gently he rested his hand over
hers, and then removed it. 'You've been under a great
deal of strain—and I realise that my behaviour has
contributed to that. I wanted to apologise to you.'

She smiled. 'It's not that—it's nothing to do with
you. It's not even because of my stepfather and the
will.' She hesitated. 'It's just that ... sometimes it's so
horrible, not remembering. Having bits and pieces of
your past handed out to you by other people. Scraps of
information. A piece here, a piece there. Discovering
they knew things they never even told you about—oh,
for your own good, because they had your best interests
at heart!' She gave a bitter laugh. 'Discovering about
yourself, from ... from charts and tests, and old
records—and things people let drop by mistake. It's
hateful,' she finished passionately, 'hateful. Sometimes
it makes me feel as if I'm going mad.'

He had listened to her gravely, his clever and
perceptive eyes never leaving her face. 'Have you told
your doctor this?'

'I've tried once or twice. He just switched me to a
different brand of tranquillisers ... I've stopped taking
them now.' She shrugged. 'He was probably right, you
see. A few days without my fix and I start weeping on
strangers' shoulders in pubs ...'

She smiled at him wanly, and he laughed softly, the
laughter lighting his eyes, and transforming them.

'Well, you weren't quite weeping on my shoulder—though I have no objection if you should feel inclined. It's quite a broad shoulder. And I'm not exactly a stranger, I hope.'

'No—no, you're not.' Isobel looked up at him. 'But all the same—there's no reason why I should burden you with all this. It's not your concern.'

'I could make it my concern.' His voice was light in tone, but his eyes were serious. 'When you say that you're given—scraps of information—what do you mean exactly? You mean you feel you've been shielded from things—things you ought to have known?'

Isobel looked away. She would have liked, then, to have told him, and she knew she could not.

'I feel sometimes as if—as if I'd been given a picture, and everything in it cohered and aligned. And then I saw it wasn't a picture, it was a jig-saw—and some of the pieces were the wrong way round, and some of them didn't fit ... and, oh, I don't know.' She sighed. 'That's a bad analogy. You were quite right last night when you said that about veils and doors and shutters. However you try to describe it, it ends up a cliché. But I mind!' She swung round to him passionately. 'I mind very much. It's my past! I want to remember it—I want it to come back.'

She stopped abruptly. She knew what she had almost said; she had managed to change it at the last moment. She had nearly said—I want *him* to come back. Her eyes widened; for a moment she hardly saw Eliot's face.

'Then why don't you look for it?'

He spoke quietly, his eyes never leaving her face. Isobel blinked, and the room came back into focus.

'I'm sorry—what did you say?'

'I said why don't you look for it?' he repeated patiently. 'Had that idea not occurred to you?'

'Look for it?' She stared at him blankly. 'How? Where?'

'Well,' he began slowly, his voice flat, 'you could start by going back to the place where it happened, couldn't you? To your old home. To the place where the accident happened.'

Isobel gave a low cry. 'I could! Of course I could! I hadn't thought of that. You see, my stepfather would never have allowed it. He hated me even to talk about what happened——'

'He can hardly prevent you now,' he said drily, with a touch of venom in his voice. His words brought Isobel up short. It was true, she realised. She was free— suddenly she felt amazingly free. To be able to go anywhere, to do anything, and not endlessly to have to account for her actions. . . . Maybe it was wrong to feel like that, but she couldn't help it. Impulsively she reached across and touched his hand.

'Thank you,' she said warmly. 'How clever you are! I think you're right. I think I might do that.'

He stood up with a dry smile. 'Glad to be of assistance. Maybe—if I get bored with banking—I could take up a third profession. Counselling, perhaps, do you think that would work? Now, come on—we'd better go. They want to close up, I think.'

'Wait—I mustn't forget this.' Isobel grabbed a sandwich.

They went outside. The swan was waiting patiently, and Isobel, who felt obscurely grateful to him, duly rewarded him for his wait.

They stopped off on the way home, and went for a short walk as he had suggested, across some fields powdered with frost, into a small copse of birch trees.

There was a magnificent view from there, across the hills of the Cotswolds, over the Malvern hills to the mountains of Wales. Isobel looked, and drew in deep breaths of the cold air. The wind was burning colour into her cheeks; she felt suddenly transformed, reinvigorated, and in a way she could not remember feeling before, confident.

Eliot said very little as they walked. He said nothing now, but seemed deep in thought. His eyes scanned the distant horizon, but Isobel felt he did not truly look at the view. She looked up at him cautiously, at the hard-etched profile, dark against the pale grey of the sky; at the black hair, which the wind lifted, and then let fall against his forehead.

'Tell me,' she said curiously, as they turned to walk back to the car, 'you said "third profession". What was the first—weren't you always a banker?'

'No,' he said shortly. 'I read for the bar. I practised as a barrister until the circumstances we spoke of last night. Naturally, after that . . .' He shrugged.

'Of course—I'm sorry, I didn't think—I shouldn't have mentioned it.'

'It doesn't matter.' He took her arm to guide her past the deep ruts in the path. 'I told you I preferred to cut myself off from the past—but of course, it's not always possible.'

'Do you feel bitter?' Isobel stopped suddenly, and turned to him, her eyes looking up into his. 'Because of what happened? It must have broken up your whole life.'

'It certainly did that.' His eyes were guarded.

Isobel hesitated. She sensed that, when he wanted, he could put an impenetrable barrier around himself, and she feared rebuff. But he had helped her, and she wanted to know more. 'Why didn't she speak out—the woman?' she burst out. 'No matter what you felt or thought—if you *did* nothing that you were accused of—why didn't she come forward, and say so?'

'You would have to ask her that,' he answered coldly, 'I have no idea. It's getting cold. Shall we go back to the car?'

He turned, and they walked back down the slope towards the road in silence. Once or twice Isobel glanced surreptitiously, but he kept his face averted from her, and the hard profile told her nothing. She wanted to speak out, to question him further, yet didn't quite dare to. When they reached the car, summoning all her courage at last, she swung round to him and looked up into his face.

'You *are* bitter,' she said impulsively. 'I sensed it the

first moment I met you—and, and yet—you were very kind to me just now. I wish—there was something that could help.'

'Wishing changes nothing, unfortunately.' He leaned forward and unlocked the door, his voice dismissive.

'Do you still love her?'

The question was spoken almost before it was formed in her mind. It seemed to spring from her lips of its own accord, and for a moment the words hung in the cold silent air. Isobel stared at him, appalled by what she had said, appalled by her own lack of tact. Eliot's eyes darkened; his knuckles stood out white against the door of the car.

'I hate her,' he said slowly. His voice was cold, almost without inflection. 'And if I met her again I should set out to destroy her one way or another.' He opened the car door. 'Shall we go?'

It snowed during the night. In the morning, when Isobel drew back the curtains and looked out over the gardens, they were transformed. Where there had been paths, and lawns, and carefully separated flower beds, there was now one sheet of glittering white; in a night all the familiar routes and pathways had disappeared. The tall yew hedges that surrounded the rose gardens, and which were usually so dark and so forbidding, reminding her always of a prison, had gone. Now they were thickly crusted with snow; they too glittered and refracted the sudden brilliance of light.

She thought then, as she had constantly that night, of Eliot Richardson, and of what he had said. *Wishing changes nothing, unfortunately . . .*

He was right, of course. She had thought then, *this man is destroying himself—does he know that?* But she had said nothing, and afterwards, late at night, unable to sleep, it had occurred to her that he and she were alike. Was she not destroying herself too—constantly striving to find a past that always eluded her? They were both of them, in their different ways, locked in the past, she saw that now. And that fact now filled her with impatience and anger. She wanted to be free of it, she thought longingly, free of it once and for all—and she would like him to be free too, because now he was like a man still serving a sentence.

She turned away from the window, and slowly, thoughtfully, her mind far away, she went through the mechanics of washing and dressing. Just for an instant when she had been with him in his apartment, and again the previous day when they had walked among the birch trees, she had felt a taste of freedom. Had he felt that? she wondered. Then, just then, fleetingly, she had been so full of thoughts of the future, incoherent thoughts that took no proper shape, but which were connected to him, that the past had slipped away. When he had kissed her, then ... something had happened, and she knew it, if she could not define it. It was as if her heart had been still for years, and suddenly it pulsed again, and the blood coursed through her veins. It was like waking from a long sleep. It was like standing on a mountain and seeing a world at her feet. It was like ... she didn't know what it was like. It was just itself, and she knew it was no good trying to explain it or analyse it or account for it. There it was.

She stared at her pale face for a moment in the glass. He had said he might call in on her today, before he went back to London, and she knew that if she was truthful that simple fact filled her with a crazy exultant happiness. She stared at her reflection. I mustn't, she thought confusedly. Mustn't like him too much. Hope for anything. Think of being in love. Think of his kisses, and his kindness. I mustn't ...

Quickly she turned away from the glass, determined to be resolute and practical. That would bring her to her senses quickly enough. First, she would go and see John Shaw, and then she would go to her stepfather's bank in the village and try and borrow from them the money that Bobby needed. Then she would go through her stepfather's belongings with Bernice, as they had planned. Bernice was leaving that day: the moment could not be put off any longer.

No more dreaming, she thought, with a wry lift of the lips.

And of course, she was right; practicality helped.

By ten she was in John Shaw's office. By ten-thirty they had completed all the arrangements that needed to be made. By eleven she was in the bank manager's office. To her own astonishment, the interview went well. Maybe asking for loans got easier the more often you did it, she thought wryly, as she heard herself put her request clearly and concisely and—she thought—a great deal more convincingly than she had put it to Eliot Richardson. But then this man was not intimidating in the least. He was small, bespectacled, formal and yet slightly avuncular. He heard her out, asked what seemed to her remarkably few questions, and then announced that, yes, he would need to talk to John Shaw, but on the whole he thought he could say the bank's attitude would be favourable.

Colour flooded into Isobel's face. She sprang to her feet impulsively. 'Oh, thank you—thank you,' she said warmly. 'You don't know—I can't tell you, the relief! I've been terribly worried . . .'

He smiled again, and the light glanced against his spectacles. Gently he explained that of course there were various formalities, papers to be drawn up and signed, but it would all take no more than a few days. He made an appointment to see her a week later, and Isobel left feeling as if she were dancing on air.

Bobby had been right after all! It wasn't so difficult! She felt proud of her success, and excited, and tried to telephone Bobby at once. But Bobby had checked out of her New York hotel, leaving no contact number . . . Isobel hung up. It didn't matter. Bobby must have gone on to Barbados earlier than expected. She would ring eventually—and when she did Isobel would be able to give her the good news.

She raced upstairs to her stepfather's rooms, a new spring in her step. Bernice looked up as she burst in, and smiled.

'Well,' she said. 'And what's been happening to you, I'd like to know? You look like a new person.'

'I feel a new person.' Isobel stopped, collected herself. Bernice was bending over a pile of her stepfather's suits and shirts. She hesitated. 'I don't know,' she said eventually. 'Everything was going so wrong, and now at last something seems to be going right, that's all.'

'Anything to do with that Mr Richardson?' Bernice's smile broadened. 'He drove you back from London, I hear.'

Isobel turned away quickly. 'No—nothing to do with him. Just business things.'

'I see.' Bernice's tone was meaningful and openly disbelieving. She sat back on her heels. 'So you feel up to doing all this? It's the worst part, this, the clearing up. But once it's done, in my experience, people feel a whole lot better.'

'We'll do it together,' Isobel said firmly. 'I was dreading it, but now—well, it has to be done, doesn't it?'

They broke for sandwiches and coffee at noon, and then Bernice looked at her watch. She sighed.

'There's just his desk now,' she said, 'he always kept the key in his pocket. I've left it on the table over there . . .' She paused. 'I thought you'd want to do that yourself. And I ought to get packed up if I'm going to catch the three-fifteen.'

Isobel looked up and touched her hand warmly.

'Of course. Thank you, Bernice. I'll finish the rest . . .' She hesitated awkwardly. 'I shall miss you, you know.'

Bernice smiled. 'I'll write. I'm going to take a bit of a break, then the agency says there'll be a job for me. But you'll keep in touch—and you'll look after yourself?'

'Of course. And Bernice—thank you. Thank you for everything.' She stood up, and they embraced warmly.

When Bernice had gone Isobel turned slowly to the bureau, picked up the key, and slowly unlocked it.

It was a large, upright writing desk, its upper cupboards lined with books behind glass doors. She remembered it from her earliest childhood. All those interviews in this room! The end-of-term school reports carefully and methodically discussed, and then filed away in one of these drawers. The medical reports, the passports. One desk: a family's history.

The three lower drawers did not take long to go through. Her stepfather had always been an orderly man, and all the papers were carefully docketed and filed. Isobel packed them into boxes methodically. Birth certificates; marriage certificates, medical cards, an envelope of cuttings about Bobby's meteoric career. . . . She glanced at each quickly and packed them away. She would look at them properly later on, she thought. She knew it would distress her to do so now.

She opened the desk flap at last. There, there were a number of small drawers and pigeonholes, but to her relief she saw that most of them were almost empty. Pens that no longer worked; erasers; paper clips. An old gold watch with a faded face that she remembered being shown as a child, and which had belonged to Edward St Aubyn's mother. An envelope with scratchy old-fashioned writing on the outside, and, inside, three locks of soft children's hair. Isobel bit her lip; whose hair? Edward's parents? Their parents? There was no way of knowing. She felt tears prick behind her eyes, and forced herself to go on.

There was one last little drawer, locked. She found the tiny key that fitted it at the back of one of the pigeonholes, and carefully drew it open. It held only a few things: a Christmas card drawn by herself, and given to her stepfather when she had been little. A bundle of faded letters tied up with blue ribbon, addressed to her stepfather in her mother's handwriting. She held them a moment, brushing the dust from them, and then quickly packed them away. There were a few postcards and some dog-eared photographs, mostly of people she could not identify—friends from her stepfather's youth, she judged, looking at the clothes, the jaunty college blazers, the plus-fours, the Oxford bags. Then one photograph caught her attention. She paused, smoothed it out, and held it closer to the light.

It had been taken in the garden in Devon, she recognised it. It was summer; a group of people were having what looked like an elaborate picnic on the lawns. Her stepfather; her mother; Bobby and herself.

She peered more closely, feeling her skin grow cold. She and Bobby looked about twelve; there were four other people in the picture—a man and a woman and two boys. Her mouth dry, she stared at the faded print. The man was sitting next to her mother; her mother's head was turned; she was looking up at him, and laughing. His wife was lying back in one of the old wooden garden chaise-longues, one hand resting listlessly in her lap, the other trailing on the grass. In front of them knelt the two boys; one, aged about fourteen, was looking at the camera directly. The other, the elder, was also looking at the camera, his face caught in a furious scowl. Her hand trembled, and she dropped the photograph.

It was Julius. Julius, his brother Edmund, and his parents. She had known it at once, and now, with a low gasp, she bent to retrieve the photograph, to scan it again. It was shadowy, not completely in focus. She had no memory of the day it pictured—none. She herself was sitting cross-legged on the far side of the picture. A little girl with her dark hair cut in a neat straight fringe, and her head turned. She was looking at Julius.

She raised the photograph closer to her eyes and stared at it in desperation. It was him. It was him. His image, at last, and it told her nothing. He was tall; dark hair fell across his brow. A book lay on the grass beside him.

She trembled, feeling suddenly a wild irrational anxiety, a wish to tear up the photograph. But she steadied herself; she knew she would regret it always if she gave in to the impulse.

Quickly she pushed it into an envelope with the other pictures, and put it into one of the boxes. What had she expected, after all? That a piece of paper would bring her memory back? Bring him back? *Wishing changes nothing, unfortunately*: that was what Eliot Richardson had said, and he had been right.

Quickly, wanting now only to finish what she had to do and leave this room and the memories it did and did not bring back, she pulled out the few remaining objects in the drawer. A sheaf of letters she had written home from school. A smaller sheaf from Bobby. There was no need to look at them now . . . she leaned across to place them on the top of the last box, and as she did so, a postcard fluttered out.

She picked it up, hardly looking at it, and then she recognised her own writing, and stopped. The words, addressed to her stepfather, leapt before her eyes.

By the time you receive this, she read, *I shall have moved on. Please do not try to locate me. I am safe and happy. I will return soon.*

Isobel stared at the card confusedly. She turned it over—a picture of some white buildings, a square, all very bright under a brilliant blue sky. The buildings looked French. She flicked the card back. *Place de la Révolution, Oran, Algérie*, she read, printed in the corner of the card. There was a foreign stamp, and an illegible postmark.

She turned the card over again, then back again, staring at it in disbelief. Algeria? She had never been to Algeria in her life; she had never even heard of Oran. And the message—what did that mean? Where was she moving on? Why had she asked her stepfather not to try and locate her? It made no sense, none at all, and yet she knew she must have written it, and that meant—could only mean—one thing. In those two years, the lost two years, she had not stayed in Devon as she had been told and had believed. She had been abroad—to Algeria. To North Africa.

They had lied to her, then—her stepfather had lied. She gave a low cry of despair. Was it never to end, this uncertainty, this unknowing? What else had happened in those two years?

She held the postcard tight against her chest, and

then, fighting back the tears of anger and frustration, she slammed the desk shut and ran from the room.

Just then all she could think of was that she couldn't bear to be there any longer, locked away with the past, a past that made no sense. She raced along the landing, and down the stairs, two at a time, and then, suddenly, came to an abrupt halt. The long-case clock in the hall struck three. Beside it, standing looking up at her, was Eliot Richardson.

'I see. May I look at that?'

He was standing before the fire in the drawing-room, immensely tall, wearing another of those impeccably cut black suits. Now he lifted one long narrow hand, palm upward, and held it out to her.

Isobel hesitated. She already regretted having said anything, having—in her shock and confusion—blurted out her discovery to this cool, unpredictable, self-contained man. Then, as his eyes met hers, he smiled, gently, and with an unexpected warmth, and all her regrets fell away. She was glad she had told him, glad that he was there. Slowly she lifted her hand and gave him the scrap of pasteboard. As he took it his fingers brushed hers.

He looked at it in silence, his head bent. He turned it over, read her message, examined it closely. The silence seemed to Isobel to go on for ever. At length he looked up, His face was still, and grave.

'You were safe. And happy.' He gave an odd smile. 'That's something at least.'

'It's nothing! Nothing!' Isobel turned away bitterly. 'I can't believe I wrote it. If it wasn't for the evidence of my own eyes I wouldn't believe it.'

'It brings back nothing—you're sure of that?' His voice was quiet.

Isobel shook her head. There was another silence. Carefully Eliot put the photograph down on a table. 'I came here today,' he began slowly, 'to make a suggestion. This just makes me even more sure it was the right suggestion.'

'A suggestion?' Isobel lifted her face to his. Her pulse quickened.

'I told you, if your past won't come back to you, you should go and look for it. You should go back to Devon, back to the place where the accident happened.'

He paused, and Isobel felt an odd sense of disappointment.

'And I should come with you.' His eyes met hers for a second, as if he expected some interruption from her, some protest. Her heart gave a sudden astonishing leap; she said nothing, and Eliot turned away, his voice dry.

'I was going to suggest that I could take some time off for a few days. And it's too long since I was back there anyway. I could drive you down. We could stay at my house, and I could try to help you.'

'Stay at your house?'

'It's perfectly all right. There's a housekeeper—staff. No need to worry about proprieties. I think it's something you should do, and I don't like the thought of your doing it alone, that's all. We could leave tomorrow if you agree.'

Isobel stared at him. His face was impassive, his manner brisk and businesslike. Yet for some reason she could not understand she felt at once grateful, excited and alarmed.

'Why are you doing this?' She raised her face to his curiously, searching his eyes, but they told her nothing.

'Why not?' He shrugged. 'Maybe I feel that I owe you something.'

'Because of the will? The house?' She stared at him, puzzled by a slight darkness that had crept into his tone.

'Who knows?' He smiled suddenly. 'Because of your eyes, perhaps. Because when you look at me like that, I find I possess chivalrous feelings after all—not something I had—expected.'

He hesitated, and Isobel looked up at him uncertainly. For some reason she thought he was deliberately turning the conversation, that the compliment was also an evasion, and designed to mislead.

And yet he was looking at her with apparent admiration, his eyes falling from her face to her figure, then quickly back to her face in a way that made her remember, sharply, the taste of his mouth on hers, the brush of his lips against her skin. Colour flooded up into her cheeks; Eliot took her arm. Lightly he tilted her face up to his.

'Say yes . . . I want you to.'

'Yes.' Her lips felt dry. She spoke the word softly.

'Good.' For a moment his grip on her arm tightened slightly, then he released her and stepped back. He looked at his watch. 'I'll have to leave you now. Can you be ready early in the morning? About eight? I don't want to leave too late in case there's more snow . . .' He paused. 'Have you thought any more about the loan you need? I wanted to ask you . . .'

'It's all right. I saw the bank in the village this morning. They've agreed to lend me the money.'

Isobel spoke quickly. Eliot gave a dry smile.

'I'm glad. Surprised, but glad. Glad for you, of course, but also for me. I'd rather you weren't in my debt.'

'Why?' She looked at him curiously.

'Because debts come between people, that's why. Now . . .' He turned back to the door. 'I'll see you at eight tomorrow. Bring plenty of warm clothes, it's bound to be freezing there. Oh—and bring your passport, can you?'

'My passport?' Isobel stared at him blankly. All this was happening too fast for her.

Eliot grinned. 'But of course. If we draw a blank in Devon, then we'll just have to try elsewhere, won't we? North Africa, for instance.'

It was a good exit line, Isobel thought wryly, and he shut the door behind him right on cue. She sank back wearily into a chair, feeling again that pulse of excitement and alarm. Was she doing the right thing, letting a man like Eliot into her life? Not that it would be exactly easy to keep him out, she reflected. The man was like a whirlwind, and although she did not know him well, the force of his will left her reeling. Cold or charming; haughty or kind—whichever side of himself he chose to project, one thing was certain. Eliot Richardson was a man used to getting his way. That he could be ruthless she had no doubt—and yet, she liked him.

And trusted him, her mind added. She sighed. It was a long time, an eternity it seemed, since she had trusted anyone, including herself.

Promptly at eight, Eliot arrived to collect her. It was already snowing and Isobel, watching anxiously for him from the window, stared when she saw him jump from the car and run towards the house. He was dressed so completely differently: a leather flying jacket lined with sheepskin, heavy boots, dark woollen trousers cut like a Cossack's and tucked into the boots. The clothes emphasised his height, the strength and muscularity of his build; today there was no trace of the smooth assured City man. He looked powerful, and he looked dangerous.

She had taken some trouble with her own appearance, tucking up her long thick hair beneath a fur hat that covered her brow and drew attention to the astonishing blue of her eyes. She was wrapped in a long black coat which emphasised the pallor of her skin, and the clarity of her complexion. When she opened the door to him, Eliot stared at her as she had stared at him, and the frank admiration in his dark eyes brought the colour winging to her cheeks. He took her gloved hand, and held it for a moment between his, his eyes never leaving her face. Then, abruptly, saying nothing, he turned away, picked up her case, put it into the boot, and helped her into the car.

He glanced at her sideways, as he accelerated smoothly away, and smiled.

'You should have warned me—I had no idea I was collecting a Russian Princess this morning. I feel I ought to sweep you on to a horse and ride off across the Steppes . . .'

'You're dressed for it too,' Isobel murmured, and Eliot laughed.

'Sheer practicality. It's going to be damned cold. We'll have to drive across the moor—I just hope it's not drifting yet, that's all.'

The journey was a long one, and the road conditions slowed them, but it seemed to Isobel to pass only too quickly. She felt happy, she realised, insulated in the warmth and quiet of the powerful car, able to look at Eliot, whose attention was occupied with the road ahead. He played some music, and they talked companionably. Isobel relaxed. It was odd, she thought to herself. He seemed cold at first, yet he could be so easy to talk to.

Once they crossed the county border into Devon, and turned off the motorway, she began to look at her surroundings more closely. The roads narrowed and became more winding, their high hedges thick with snow. Eliot glanced at her.

'You recognise it?'

'Yes.' She hesitated. 'That last village we passed through—we used to shop there sometimes on market day. My stepfather's house was about three or four miles from here. Look, there's the turning to the village. Aston Deverall . . .'

Eliot glanced up at the signpost, and accelerated past the turning.

'Not today.' Her hands clenched involuntarily in her lap, and he reached across and touched them gently. 'Tomorrow perhaps—if you feel up to it. Today we'll just go on to my house, I think. You can rest—we'll have dinner, make plans, sit in front of the fire—would you like that?'

'Very much.' Isobel smiled at him shyly, and Eliot removed his hand.

'I should warn you, my housekeeper will be extremely curious. She's a great matchmaker. I've never brought a woman down to the house before, and I'm afraid she'll jump to all the wrong conclusions.'

He paused, as if expecting Isobel to say something. But she was too busy wrestling with her own idiot mind, which at once wished that the housekeeper's conclusions might not be so wrong. She glanced quickly away out of the window. Whatever was the matter with her? That was the last thing she ought to be thinking now.

'So just ignore all the hints, all right? I'll try and protect you from the visits to the old nurseries and the heavy sighs over the ancestral cradle. She looked after my uncle, you see, and she's known me since I was a boy. She tried for years to marry me off and—look.' He broke off suddenly. 'We'll have to take one of the Dartmoor roads—and that was where it happened, wasn't it? You won't mind? It won't upset you?'

'No.' Isobel shook her head.

'Fine. It's the next turning. We'll have to watch the road. It's not often used, and it may be icy . . .'

It seemed to Isobel that he had grown tense, and his tension grew more marked as they turned down the tiny road he had indicated. He gripped the steering wheel tightly; his eyes never left the road. Once or twice, as their wheels slid on ice, he swore softly. Isobel looked at him curiously.

They had reached a pair of tall wrought-iron gates, which already stood open. Eliot spun the wheel and they turned in through them, and up a long winding drive. After about a mile they rounded a bend, and the house came into view; a long mellow façade of soft grey stone, built on a slight slope, looking down into the valley. Isobel caught her breath, and at once Eliot stopped. He turned and looked at her.

'What a lovely house . . . it's beautiful . . .'

There was a tiny silence. Looking at him she thought she saw his mouth tighten a little. He pressed the accelerator pedal again, and the car slid forward.

'It's seventeenth century, with an eighteenth century façade.' His voice was brusque. 'I'm glad you like it.'

'I like it very much—and you haven't even told me its name.'

'Stokesay. Stokesay Priory. There were monastic buildings here for centuries—that's how it got the name, I believe.' He paused. 'It's quite famous, actually. I'm surprised that—living as close as you did—you never visited it. In my uncle's day, I mean. He was in the Foreign Office and hardly ever here, so I don't suppose you would have come across him, but you might have visited the house.'

Isobel smiled. 'I wish I had. It's lovely. I'll have to make up for it now.'

He braked sharply as she spoke, pulling up in front of a wide door on which the brass gleamed. Instantly it opened, and a small plump woman with white hair came out.

'Isobel, this is Mrs Deering. Mrs Deering, Miss Latimer . . .'

Isobel felt herself regarded by a pair of sharp brown eyes. They seemed to take her in at a glance, then wavered in Eliot's direction a little uncertainly. Finally, the woman smiled.

'Come in, come in away out of the snow now, my dear. You must be tired with all that travelling, and the snow so thick—they've had the ploughs out on the valley roads the best part of the day. Come into the warm now—I'll show you up to your room.'

Isobel hesitated, glancing back at Eliot, but he waved at her to go on.

'I'll just take the car round and garage it—there's a couple of things I have to see to.' He glanced at his watch. 'Mrs Deering's sure to have made us a good dinner—it's nearly four now. We'll meet in the library for a drink, shall we? About six? Mrs Deering will show you where it is.'

With that he was gone. Slowly Isobel turned and followed the housekeeper inside, across a wide hall, up a beautiful oak staircase, along a corridor. The housekeeper was chattering all the way—about the weather, about the state of the roads, about how good it was to have Mr Eliot, as she called him, back home after all these months. She threw open the door to a bedroom, and Isobel followed her inside. A fire burned in the grate; there was a small, delicate four-poster bed hung with faded but still beautiful chintz. Isobel stopped.

'So I'll have your case brought up in a few minutes, my dear. And a cup of tea—I expect you'd like that. The bathroom is through that door there, and if you'd like to draw a bath the water's good and hot, that I do know ...' She paused. 'I'll be leaving you, then. You have everything you need?'

'Oh yes. Yes, thank you, it's lovely.' Isobel managed to get the words out, and if the housekeeper noticed anything odd in her tone she gave no sign of it, but quietly left the room. The moment she had gone, and the door was shut, Isobel gave a low moan. She pressed her hand against her forehead, covered her eyes, shut her lids tight. The room was lit only by one small lamp, but to her the light was blinding. Pain stabbed across from temple to temple. Unsteadily, she reached for a chair and leaned against it, drawing in her breath, trying to steady herself.

Eventually the light faded; the pain ebbed. Isobel set her lips, and looked across the room to the door of the bathroom, which was closed. She thought, carefully, spelling the words out to herself.

The bath is on the right, as you go in. It's a deep old-fashioned one, with claw feet and brass taps. The basin is on the left. It's shaped like a scallop shell, on a pedestal. The window is facing you. It's white glass, frosted, with blue Victorian stained glass edgings. One of the blue panes has a crack in it ...

With a low cry she ran across the room and threw back the door. The bath was on the right. The scallop basin was on the left. The window was facing her. Even from where she was standing she could see the cracked pane of blue glass.

She stood there, the colour draining from her face. It was true then. She had known it the second she entered the room.

She had been here before, more than once. Often enough to know the details of the bedroom intimately— so intimately she could have navigated it blindfold. She

raised her eyes and met those of her pale reflection in
the glass, and for the first time she felt an unease—a
shaft of suspicion.

She had been here before. Had Eliot Richardson
known that? Had his housekeeper? And if they had—
why were they lying to her?

CHAPTER FIVE

SHE dressed carefully for dinner that night, feeling obscurely that if she looked her best it would arm her in some way—though against what she was uncertain. The velvet suit she wore was dusky amethyst, the colour of African violets. The skirt was cut full to mid-calf, and emphasised her tiny waist. The jacket was Victorian in its cut, with a high collar that framed her delicate neck, sleeves full at the shoulder and tight at the wrist. Isobel looked at herself a little doubtfully. It was beautiful, the colour glowed like a jewel, but the little jacket moulded itself to her body as it had been designed to do, emphasising the full curve of her breasts, the narrow span of her waist. Under it she wore a silk shirt with a jabot that frothed at her throat in a foam of delicate lace.

It looked at once modest and erotic, so much so that she almost changed out of it again. But then she told herself not to be stupid. She was on edge, that was all—suspicious and full of imaginings. Apart from the evening when she had gone to his London flat, Eliot had behaved with total decorum towards her. She acknowledged now, as she looked at herself in the glass, that she wished it wasn't always so. She was attracted to him; she was honest enough to admit that to herself. She must put a stop to such thoughts, she decided firmly. He was acting now out of gallantry, perhaps from a delayed sense of guilt at her stepfather's will—that was all. Nervously she gathered her thick hair and twisted it up, pinning it into a formal chignon at the base of her neck. There: that looked better. She felt she could face him now.

As Eliot had promised her, Mrs Deering proved an excellent cook, and the dinner she had prepared for them was delicious. But, though Isobel enjoyed the meal, she did not feel entirely at ease. Eliot's manner

still seemed to her tense, though she thought he tried
hard to disguise it. He kept looking at her watchfully,
as course succeeded course, as if he expected some
reaction from her that she was failing to give.

And the housekeeper's manner was odd too. She
seemed unaccountably nervous. Isobel noticed that her
hand shook as she placed the dishes on the table. Once
she intercepted a glance that passed between her and
Eliot, a glance that was like a query on the
housekeeper's part. Eliot, in response, gave an almost
imperceptible shake of the head.

Finally, with irritation he sought to disguise but
which Isobel could sense, he curtailed the meal and
suggested they move to the drawing-room for coffee.

It was a beautiful room; not the large formal
drawing-room, Eliot explained briefly, that was too
large and chilly in the winter, but the room he used
when he stayed at the house. Taking her elbow, he
guided her to the fire.

The housekeeper brought them a silver tray with
coffee, and then wished them good night. Eliot brought
Isobel, unasked, a glass of brandy and then, after
pacing back and forth a little, sat down beside her and
sipped his own brandy. The room was silent except for
the spurts and flickerings of the fire. Isobel glanced at
him. He was wearing a jacket of black velvet which
emphasised the darkness of his hair; in the soft light of
the lamps the planes of his face were harsh, and his eyes
were shadowed. He seemed lost in thought for a while,
as if he wrestled with some problem in his mind.
Eventually, as if he had come at last to some decision,
he set down his glass abruptly, reached across and took
her left hand.

He lifted it, and held it between his own. Very gently,
he stroked it. Isobel sat quite still. At his touch, the
memory of his kisses leapt in her blood. She felt tongue-
tied, unable to speak, afraid of her own feelings
and even more afraid that he might sense them.
Eventually he spoke.

'If I am going to help you,' he began slowly and

deliberately, as if this speech had been rehearsed in his mind, 'then you have to tell me everything you know. You realise that, don't you, Isobel? If you leave things out—for whatever reason, because you think they have no relevance perhaps, it only makes it harder.'

'Yes—of course. I know.' Isobel looked away miserably, the colour mounting in her cheeks. She knew he was right, and that if he was going to help her she ought to tell him all she knew—such as it was!—but at the thought her mind rebelled. She couldn't tell him about the interview with the doctor—just the memory of that scene now made her sick with foreboding.

'There *is* something.' He leaned forward. 'Isobel—can't you tell me? Don't you trust me?'

She looked back at him then, and the expression in his eyes was so full of apparent concern that her heart contracted.

'I . . . I don't know.' Her mind spun wildly, sensing he was not going to give up, that she had to say something. 'I just suspect that it might not all have happened the way I was told. Obviously it didn't—the postcard proves that. But it's more than that.' She drew a deep breath to steady herself. 'You see, I was always told that everything was a series of chances. That I had gone to the party—that the man who was driving the car . . .'

'Julius.'

'Yes, Julius—that I hardly knew him.' She paused, her colour deepening. 'I don't think that's totally true.'

'You don't?' His voice was calm. One tiny muscle tightened in his cheek.

'No. I . . .' She drew in her breath and then the words came out in a rush. 'We'd known his family, you see, when I was much younger. His mother was a semi-invalid, and his father—I remember his father! They used to come to our house. The parents, and the two sons. The families were friends. And then . . . well, I think his father and my mother were in love.' She swallowed. 'I don't think they had an affair or anything—but I know he loved her, and she him—

Bobby and I both remember it. The way they used to look at each other. And then, suddenly, they stopped coming. Maybe my stepfather found out, or his wife. Maybe they just decided they had to end it all, I don't know. But there was a relationship, do you see? Julius wasn't a stranger.'

'I begin to see.' His voice was flat. Isobel, caught up now in the memories, leaned towards him impulsively.

'My stepfather wouldn't have their name mentioned in the house, and later it was the same. No one ever mentioned Julius, or his family. Every time I asked any questions I was told not to rake up the past, that he deserved to get killed and that was the end of it. And then just before my stepfather died, Bobby told me something. She said . . .' Isobel hesitated. 'She said that I'd been in love with Julius. After I left school, before the accident happened. She said—I don't know—that we met up with him and his brother Edmund somewhere, and I fell in love with him. That it was just a silly adolescent kind of crush—and Julius, of course, took no notice. He wasn't even aware of my existence. And of course, she must be right; she was there. She knows. But after she'd told me—I did wonder a little. If—if she might have been mistaken.'

He had listened to this recital carefully, his face expressionless, still holding her hand in his. Now he released it, and leaned back.

'I see,' he said slowly. 'And why did you think that, exactly?'

'Because I was in his car, and if he was so unaware of my existence that seems odd.' Her voice tightened. 'But not just that. You see—I remember him.'

'You remember Julius?' He swung round, his eyes dark against the pallor of his skin.

'I do. I always did. Not details, nothing of what happened—not even what he looked like. But I remember his eyes. He had grey eyes. I used to dream of them night after night. And the expression in his eyes—as if he hated me. It was the only memory I had, and it was so *strong*. And so . . . I think that perhaps it wasn't quite the way Bobby remembered. That something happened between Julius and me.' She hesitated, her voice low. 'He haunted me, Eliot,' she finished awkwardly. 'It sounds absurd, and I don't really believe it myself. But that's how it felt.'

'Does he haunt you still?'

The question was coolly put, interjected fast, and it took her by surprise.

'Why do you ask?'

He gave a small angry gesture of the hand, and his mouth tightened.

'Well, it's a little romantic, don't you think? Somewhat fanciful? The beautiful young woman, haunted by the ghost of a dead man, or a dead lover. Is that what you think?'

'No!' The blood washed up into her face. 'No—I never thought that. Except . . .' She broke off, still unable to bring herself to tell him, and looked away. 'You don't believe me,' she finished sadly.

Eliot sighed.

'It's not that I don't believe you,' he began cautiously, his voice neutral. 'It's just a little bewildering, that's all. And convenient—almost as if you contrived it. You remember this and you don't remember that. You were told this, and you suspected the other . . .'

A note of anger had crept into his voice, and Isobel turned to him indignantly. 'I can't help it! You asked me to tell you the truth—to explain. I knew it would be useless. You don't believe me—no one does.'

'I don't believe you totally, no.' He cut her off. 'I think . . .' His voice softened. 'I think that it's possible you could be misleading yourself. Not deliberately, I don't mean that, but obviously your mind is suppressing certain events, and there must be a reason for that. I think this whole question of—Julius, of some mysterious relationship with him, is probably just a smokescreen. Something your mind has thrown up to hide other memories, memories that unconsciously you don't *want* to remember . . .'

'That's not true!'

'Isn't it?' He swung round to her suddenly. 'Are you sure? What about relationships with other men? You're a very beautiful woman. You were nineteen when the accident happened. Are you trying to tell me there was no boyfriend, no man in your life then? I find that hard to believe. There easily could have been. You could have gone to that party with him, quarrelled, and been unwise enough to beg a lift from another man, who'd been drinking. That's a possible scenario, isn't it? After all, Bobby has no reason to lie, does she? If she says this Julius was hardly aware you existed, why not accept that?'

'Because it doesn't *feel* true! That's all. It just doesn't fit—every instinct I possess tells me it wasn't *like* that.' She broke off as she saw his face harden, and her voice faltered. 'You think I'm wrong about that?'

'I think you should ask yourself one or two other questions.' His voice was cold. 'For instance—tell me something. Since the accident—which happened five years ago, let's remember that—have you been involved with any men since then?'

Isobel stared at him, for he put the question without urgency, with a kind of cold detachment that cut her to the quick.

'I . . . no, I haven't. No one.'

'There you are, then!' A note of triumph rang in his voice. 'You've been leading an unnatural life—a sheltered life. Closeted away in a huge house with an old man who was dying—a virtual prisoner . . .'

'That's not true!'

'You've had none of the normal relationships with people your age, men your age, that a woman like you should have, needs to have. And so, of course, your mind dwells on the past. It invents aspects of it that probably never existed. It romanticises what was, in fact, a fairly straightforward sequence of events. And because you refuse to admit to yourself that something like that happened, that you were partly culpable, you weave this whole fantasy about a dead man and your relationship with him. After all, that's safe, isn't it, Isobel? An obsession with a man who just happens to be dead . . .'

Isobel stared at him white-faced. There was anger in his eyes, and a cold sarcasm in his voice. The change from the gentleness and solicitude he had shown her before was so marked, so abrupt and unexpected, that his words hurt doubly. Her throat felt tight and constricted, pain throbbed behind her eyes.

'Stop—please stop!' she said in a low voice. 'It's not true. None of what you say is true. I haven't deliberately excluded men from my life. I was ill—my stepfather needed me there. I rarely met anyone, and . . .'

'And now?' He cut across her quickly, and stepped towards her. She stared up at him, white-faced.

'Now?'

'Yes, now,' he said impatiently. 'Unless you're totally blind to my existence—which seems to be the case,' he paused, and the corner of his lips lifted in a bitter smile. 'Have you no idea what I feel—why I might have asked you down here, brought you here myself?'

'I thought . . . I thought you wanted to help me.'

'God damn it—yes, I wanted to help you. And you think that was the only reason?' His eyes held hers, and he took another step towards her. 'Obviously,' he went on, his voice softening, 'obviously you have no idea of the effect you can have on a man. You've been shut up with your stepfather for so long that you've forgotten, if you ever knew, how a man feels when he's with a woman like you. Isobel . . .' He reached out his hand to her, and Isobel flinched. His eyes darkened. 'Keep still.' Slowly he reached up one hand, and touched her throat. Isobel felt fire dart through her blood. Gently his cool fingers circled her throat, tilted her face up to his.

'What made you wear your hair like that—tonight? Did you think it made you look older? Sterner? Less desirable?' He smiled. 'Well, you were wrong. However. I prefer it—loose.'

As he spoke, with one quick movement and before Isobel could react, he deftly pulled out the comb that held her hair up, and tossed it aside. The thick hair fell in a tumble around her shoulders. Held by him, mesmerised, Isobel did not move, and, very gently, his hands tightening around the nape of her neck, he drew her to him. For a long moment he looked down into her face, searching her eyes, then, slowly and deliberately, he lowered his mouth to hers.

The warm touch of his lips sent a current that arced through her whole body with an agonising sweetness. It was only then, when the response of her body was so swift, so instantaneous, that she knew truly how much she had secretly desired his kisses, thought of them, longed for them, over the past days when he had hardly touched her. She gasped, and he drew her body against his, so she felt his heart hammer against her breast. Gently, firmly, he parted her lips, and deepened his kiss; Isobel tensed, then let her body relax softly and without resistance, against the stirring, the fierce hardening of his. He gave a ragged sigh against her mouth, as he felt her response, as her tongue sought his. His hand moved up to caress the curve of her breast where it thrust under the silk velvet, and she gave a little incoherent cry of desire. His mouth moved down to her throat, to the soft skin there.

'Not here . . .' he said thickly. 'Not here. Isobel—come with me.'

'I want you. Now. Tomorrow. Soon. When you are ready. But you have to know what I feel, how much I want you.'

He had taken her into her bedroom. Now he shut the door, and leaned against it.

'I want you so much that I can think of nothing else. It blots out everything, even the past. When I'm with you, I feel the past never happened—or most of it. Did you realise that?'

'No.'

'Then I'm better at dissembling than I thought.' He gave a grim smile. 'However, there comes a point when no man could hide what he feels, and . . .' His eyes lightened. 'Do you think,' he went on conversationally, his voice light with irony, 'do you think you could undo those buttons? There are a great many of them, and I should hate for it to get ripped . . .'

He reached out and touched her as he spoke, and Isobel trembled. Slowly she lifted her hands, and holding his gaze, undid the buttons one by one. It took some time. Eliot did not move.

'You could take it off, perhaps?'

She did so.

'That's better.' She saw his eyes fall to the jut of the nipples beneath the thin silk, and she could hear that though he kept his voice dry and calm, he did so with difficulty. 'Now. Come here.'

Slowly Isobel moved towards him. She tried to keep her eyes on his face and to shut out everything else. Behind her, in the grate, the banked fire crackled. Isobel shivered.

'Something happened when I met you.' He spoke very deliberately; at the same time he lifted his hand and touched her breast, so that Isobel gasped. 'I felt as if I knew you, and you knew me. As if, between us, the ordinary processes of—courtship, for want of a better word, were superfluous. Unnecessary.'

Slowly he moved his thumb in a soft circling movement over the tip of her breast, his eyes never leaving her face, as if he wanted to watch her reaction. Isobel felt her lips part; her blood seemed to rush through her veins with a new heavy warmth. She felt the nipple, the aureole, jut and harden beneath the touch of his hand. The deliberation with which he spoke, the apparent detachment with which his hands explored her body, simultaneously frightened her and yet heightened the eroticism of the moment. She stared at him, held by the darkness of his gaze, willing her mind to blot out everything else but the touch of his fingers, their slow stroking, and the words he spoke.

'I wanted you, first. I wanted to help you, second. You have to understand that. And so—the night you came to my flat——' He paused. 'Well, things got a little out of control for that reason. And then I found myself telling you things I had discussed with no one.

No one. That night, I couldn't sleep. I was angry with myself—frustrated too—but mostly angry. I knew you had been ill, that I should never have behaved like that. I swore to myself that I wouldn't touch you again, not unless I was sure—sure that you wanted me to. I kept to that resolve for three days—until now.'

His hand tightened around her breast, and Isobel felt herself shudder, step towards him. He smiled, a little bitterly.

'Now that I touch you again—I don't know how I managed such self-control. But having you here, seeing you here . . .' His voice broke as he said that, and his hands slipped up to the base of her throat, to the fastening of her blouse. 'Let me, Isobel—let me . . .' His voice thickened. He moved his lips to the skin of her throat, arching her back to his kiss. 'Tell me—no, don't tell me. I know. I know I have to be right . . .'

'Right?' She sighed the word against his cheek, her mind groping confusedly after the sense of his words, hardly able to think as she felt his strong hands gently part her blouse, felt with a shudder and a beating up of blood, the touch of his fingers against her bare skin. The want was so sharp and so sweet and so immediate—and so familiar, as if it were the most natural thing in the world.

'Isobel . . .' Very gently, his finger traced the pale veins in her full breasts; she glanced down, seeing his hands tanned against the alabaster pallor of her skin. She trembled. He bent his head, first to one breast, then to the other, sucking the stiffened nipples between the softness of his lips so that she cried out, and the pulse in her blood beat up stronger and stronger.

His hands circled her waist, spanned it, then moved down in a slow arching caress over the curve of her buttocks, gripping her, drawing her up against him full length so she felt the hard thrust of his flesh against her. His breathing was ragged now; she felt his heart hammer against her. He reached for her hand.

'Touch me—Isobel, touch me. Give me your hand. Feel how much I want you . . .' He raised his head from

her breasts, and his mouth came down hard on hers, so
her lips cut off his words. His hand gripped hers,
drawing it with a deep sigh against his chest, against the
hardness of his stomach, against the leap of flesh under
her fingers.

'Such a long time . . .' he murmured incoherently
against her lips. 'It has been so long . . . now.' He drew
back from her for a moment, his eyes glitteringly dark,
searching hers. With a quick impatience he loosened his
tie, reached for the fastening of his belt, then lifted his
hands again, and cupped her breasts up to him.

'Tell me . . . I want to hear you say it . . .' His fingers
touched the jutting points of her nipples, very lightly,
teasingly, so she cried out, and that moist secret
sweetness flowered in her blood. 'Tell me. Tell me you
want me, Isobel . . .'

She looked up at him, trying to focus her eyes on his
face, trying to focus her mind before the darkness of the
desire she felt engulfed it. The light in his eyes held hers
for a moment, then receded. She felt her eyelids close,
felt her body sag against his. She could hardly speak.
All she knew was that she wanted to touch his skin, to
feel it naked against hers. That she wanted to lie under
his weight, to feel the power and the thrust of him, to
feel his hand against the soft skin of her inner thigh,
touching her, stroking her, opening her to him.

'Oh, I want you so much . . .' Her voice faltered as
her mouth sought his, and the room, the world, the
planet seemed to spin away into an infinite black space.

'I want you. Julius . . .'

His mouth had already sought hers in angry triumph.
The name was spoken against his lips, his thigh was
pressed between hers. She spoke out of the dark, out of
the beat in her blood, and the pulse of her desire, unaware of what she said. And so it was only when she felt
the immediate tensing of his body, the suddenly painful
grip of his hands that she realised what she had said.

She stared at him, feeling the blood drain from her
face, her eyes wide. And she saw his face alter. In an
instant the concentration of desire had gone; he looked

down at her, his dark eyes flashing, his face a sudden
mask of cold, furious doubt. His hands tightened
involuntarily against her shoulders so that his nails bit
into her skin, and she cried out. He held her like that,
looking down at her, for what seemed like an eternity
of silence. It was as if he were waiting—for an
explanation, an apology, something that could cut
through the horrible barrier which she felt spring up
like a shield between them. Tremblingly Isobel pressed
her hand to her forehead.

'I'm sorry—I'm so sorry! I don't know why I said
that. I can't believe I did. Eliot—please believe me——'
She raised her eyes desperately to his. 'I wasn't thinking
of him—not at all. I wasn't even *thinking*. I was only
aware of you, of us. Of what . . .' Her voice broke.
'Eliot, *please* . . .'

'Forget it.' He released her abruptly, and stepped
back. His lips curled in a cold smile. 'I'm pleased you
remember my name now anyway.'

'It's not like that—it wasn't like that! Truly! I . . . I
wanted you! I don't know why I said that—how it
happened. I can't explain it . . .'

'It's a little late for explanations, in any case.' His
face had set in hard lines. He glanced down at his
watch. 'I'll leave you.' He turned to the door, and
Isobel sprang after him, reaching for his arm.

'No—wait—please don't go. Eliot—wait!'

'I think not.' He disengaged her hand coldly.
'Anything I felt . . .' He hesitated a second. 'Let's just
say that any desire I felt has just successfully been
killed stone dead. And there's no point in trying to
resurrect it now. Odd, isn't it?' Again his lips curled
in that cold smile. 'I've experienced jealousy before—but never for a dead man. Good night, Isobel.'
He hesitated, with his hand on the door. 'Sweet
dreams,' he added coldly, and then shut it firmly
behind him.

The next morning, she told him.

They were in the car, high up on the moors, surrounded by snow. His manner, as it had been at breakfast, was cool, businesslike, calm. Suddenly, unable to bear it any longer, Isobel turned to him pleadingly. 'Eliot, stop the car. Now, please. I must talk to you.'

'As you wish.'

He pulled in to the side of the road, and switched off the engine. He let his hands rest on the wheel, apparently relaxed, apparently unworried. Fixedly Isobel stared at his hands in their black leather gloves. She knew she dared not look at his face, and that if she did so, she would never get through it. Her throat felt parched and tight; she had to force each word out.

'There's something I didn't tell you. I realise now that I should have done. The day you collected me in London, I had been to see a doctor—a new doctor. A specialist.'

Haltingly, the words seeming to drop into the great silence like pebbles tossed into dark water, she told him what had happened, what the doctor had said. He heard her out, in silence, never prompting her, never helping her, even when her voice faltered, and she fell quiet, and then had to force herself to go on. Hesitatingly she moved on to their arrival at his house, to the familiarity of her room there, the strong sense she had had that she had been there before. Then, her story looping back in her embarrassment and distress, to the doctor again.

'He warned me, you see,' she ended. 'He told me he thought that my memory might be coming back, that it might be triggered by something, particularly if, after all this time, I was to be physically involved with a man. And so, I think, I suppose—last night . . .'

'Yes?' For the first time he turned to her, his voice still cold.

'Well, that must account for it, mustn't it?' She raised her eyes pleadingly to his. 'There's no other explanation. I wasn't thinking of the past then, not at all. I want you to believe that—that's why I had to tell you this. So— so you might understand. I couldn't help what I said. I know it wasn't rational, and I wish—oh God, I wish it hadn't happened.'

'Don't cry. There's no need.'

He had not even turned his head, so he must have heard her quiet tears rather than seen them. There was silence for a while, as Eliot stared out over the snow. Eventually, he turned to her.

'Why didn't you tell me before? I asked you last night. I told you then—if I were to help you, you had to tell me everything . . .'

'I don't know. I was embarrassed, ashamed . . .'

'Ashamed to have had a lover?' His voice hardened. 'Is that so terrible an admission in this day and age?'

'Of course not—no!' She swung round to him. 'But not to know who he was—not even to know how it happened! You can't imagine how horrible that is. The doctor said—he said it could have been rape. They couldn't rule out that possibility, that was why they kept it from me for so long. The injuries I had— they might not have been caused by the accident alone. They didn't know. I don't know . . .'

Her voice had risen in distress. Eliot turned to her and looked at her carefully. His voice was icy.

'You think you were raped? By—Julius? Is that what you're saying?'

'No! I don't think that. I can't. When I think of him I don't associate him with threat—not at all. And the doctor in London thought that theory was wrong. He said that if that had happened I would have other symptoms, that I would be afraid of men. That I wouldn't want to be touched . . .' She broke off, and looked away. 'And you must know I don't feel that.'

She paused. He was gazing out over the snow again, his fingers drumming lightly on the steering-wheel. Isobel longed to reach out to him, to touch him, but she did not dare. She bent her head.

'Perhaps,' he began at last, slowly, 'you had more than one lover. Has that thought occurred to you? After all, you say now that you don't associate this Julius with threat. Last night, you said you remembered the expression of his eyes—that it was as if he hated you. Perhaps that was why. Or maybe he was jealous because you preferred another man. Really, when one comes to consider it, the possibilities are endless. And the way you insist on concentrating on that one man doesn't help . . .'

'You don't believe me.' Isobel cut him off, and sank her face in her hands. 'You don't—oh, I can't bear it . . .'

'Well, you must admit it's a little difficult.' He turned back to her, his voice dry. 'Your story changes all the time. How do I know there isn't more you haven't told me? My house, for instance. When we arrived there you were quite certain you didn't know it, had never been there. Today you tell me you recognised your room immediately you went into it—yet last night you said nothing. Why? There was nothing to be ashamed of there, presumably.'

'I don't *know* why I didn't tell you at once.' Miserably Isobel turned her face away. 'Maybe I've been used to keeping silent so long, always feeling that people were telling me half-truths. And maybe I don't trust myself any more either. I can't trust my own mind—it plays tricks on me, and . . .' She turned back to him impulsively, and reached gently for his arm. 'But I promise you now, Eliot, I swear to you I've told you everything. All I know, you know. There are no more secrets between us.'

'I'd like to believe you. I wonder if you're right.'

For a second his hand rested over hers, and he looked into her eyes. She saw his mouth twist slightly, ironically, and she knew he was still not convinced, though his face had softened. Isobel cleared her throat and removed her hand.

'Perhaps I should go home,' she suggested quietly. 'Everything you've said is true. I can't blame you—why should you go on with this? I can see now . . .' She hesitated, choosing her words carefully, anxious only to make it easy for him to say what she dreaded to hear. 'I can see that now you probably feel rather differently about me. And that's quite all right. I understand. I can move out—get a train back—whatever . . .'

He reached across to her suddenly, and forced her round to face him. 'You think because of what you've just told me that my attitude has changed?' His lips lifted at the corners. 'That because your past is a little more—dramatic—physically than you thought, that I'm going to drop you? Is that what you think?'

Isobel did not answer him, but the slow colour mounted in her cheeks. Eliot's face softened, and very gently he laid one finger on her lips.

'My sweet idiot, I think you don't know me very well. I think you didn't listen to what I said last night. And I think if you mention leaving again in that noble self-sacrificing manner, I shall become very angry indeed. So—don't. All right?'

Very gently he pressed his lips against hers, and then drew back.

'After all,' he went on, his voice becoming more cheerful, 'there is a positive side to this—had you realised that?'

'A positive side?' Isobel stared at him. His eyes glinted with amusement.

'But of course,' he said smoothly. 'If your doctor thinks that making love may trigger your memory, I have a perfect excuse, don't you think? I can make love to you in the hope it might be therapeutic. I shall have other motives as well, no doubt, at the time. But still . . .' Slowly he lifted his hand, and cupped her face up to his. 'That is—if you still want your memory back. Do you?'

The way he inflected the question made Isobel's lips curve in an answering smile. 'Yes,' she began.

'Then I can't think of a more pleasurable way of releasing it—can you?'

His mouth came down on hers. Instantly Isobel felt the old want for him arc through her blood. She parted her lips to the thrust of his tongue, as he clasped her tight in his arms. He kissed her in a new way then, without tenderness, with a sweet savagery, as if he meant to force her to acknowledge once and for all the need that flamed from his body to hers. When, at last, he released her, she shuddered against him, letting her face fall against his shoulder. He held her very tight, his breath coming quickly; then, as abruptly as he had pulled her to him, he released her.

'Later,' he said. 'What I have in mind for us would be a great deal more pleasurable if we weren't in the front of a car with damn stupid gear levers and brakes to entangle us. For now ...' He drew in his breath, and looked at her in mock reproof as, cheeks aflame, Isobel sank back against her seat. 'Now, if you could look a little less wanton, so I can keep my mind on the business in hand—I think we should stick to the plan I made for this morning. You agree?'

'I agree.' Isobel smiled ruefully. 'I may not want to agree, but I'm sure you're right.'

'And you can cut that out too,' he growled. 'When you pretend to be demure it's exceedingly inflammatory—as I'm sure you're well aware. So,' he reached forward and started the engine, 'we'll continue as planned. We'll drive past your old house, and then up to the road where the accident happened. Yes? You feel ready to do that? It won't upset you?'

At the sudden gentleness that came back into his voice, Isobel felt her heart dance. She nodded silently.

Eliot began to ease the car carefully back on to the road, and Isobel rested her flushed face against the cool glass of the window. For the first time for months she felt a great and startling happiness, a sudden freedom of soul. It wasn't just that she trusted him, she thought; it wasn't just that she liked him, strange, and frightening and unpredictable, though he could be.

She loved him.

It was a relief not to dissemble to herself any more. Her heart danced with happiness. Beside that fact, everything else receded into unimportance.

She looked out over the blinding white of the snow, and felt the same clear dazzling light animate all her senses. Such light, such clarity, such equilibrium after years of darkness and blindness. *I love him, and I shall tell him*, she thought. *Not yet, not quite yet. But soon.*

CHAPTER SIX

'NOTHING? You're sure?'

The light was beginning to fade; as the sun sank behind low clouds on the horizon the snow took on a bluish shadow. Isobel shivered. A wind had started up, and she felt very cold.

'I recognised the house, yes. As I said.' She hesitated. Eliot took her arm, as they stood by the car, and she looked along the road before them. They were on the lower slopes of the moor. Here a line of stunted trees, their outline distorted by years of savage weather and high winds, leaned across the road, their branches almost interlaced above their heads. The road itself was narrow and winding, with deep ditches on either side. Ahead of them, in the twilight, Isobel could just make out the road sign that marked the crossroads.

'And here?'

His voice was soft, the pressure of his arm against hers very slight.

'I know this must be the road. They told me where it happened, and this is the right place . . .' She hesitated. 'The trees, the ditches, the crossroads—it's just as I was told.'

'And?'

'And—nothing.' She sighed. 'It brings back nothing. Eliot—I'm sorry. It isn't working.'

'It doesn't matter.' His voice was firm, businesslike. He shrugged, then turned to lead her back to the car. 'I was probably being simplistic—and over-optimistic. There's no reason why it should work, just like that.' He too sighed, and she thought she heard an odd note of bitterness and disappointment in his voice. 'We tried, that's the important thing. And now the light's going, and it's getting cold. Come on—we'd better make for home before it's dark.'

He started the drive back along a different road from the one they had taken earlier, driving slowly, the headlamps illuminating the thick snow, which was already beginning to freeze over. Eliot was quiet and thoughtful; beside him, Isobel too sat quietly, trying to force her mind to tussle with the past. She felt tired, and disappointed. Somehow, earlier in the day, she had felt so optimistic—the happiness that being with Eliot made her feel had spilled over into a sense of general well-being: she had been almost certain, she realised now, that *something* would come back to her—when she saw the house where she spent her childhood—when they visited the scene of the accident above all.

She turned thoughtfully to Eliot. 'I suppose there's more I could do. Perhaps, as you say, it was foolish to think it would be so simple—just to visit these places.'

Eliot glanced at her. 'Something more?'

'Well, yes. For instance, it would have been impossible before, and my stepfather would never have allowed it. But now—since you brought me here, it occurred to me that it would be quite simple to make enquiries locally, don't you think?'

He didn't answer, and she pressed on, warming to the idea. 'After all, there must be people living down here still who remember the accident. If I talked to them—someone might remember something, something I hadn't been told. And then . . .' She glanced at him. 'There's Edmund. Julius's brother. He must still be alive. If I could trace him—if he would talk to me . . .'

She was pleased by the idea, and had quite expected some warm endorsement. To her surprise, the suggestion was met with stony silence. His mouth tightened; the wheels of the car slid slightly on the icy road, and Eliot swore. Isobel looked at him.

'You don't think that's a good idea?'

He shrugged dismissively. 'Not particularly. Why do you imagine he would help?'

'Well, he was there that night—Bobby said so. He must remember something. And Bobby said Edmund was much the nicer of the two brothers—that he was gentle, kind—she liked him, she said so.'

'Oh, well, if he has Bobby's good word, of course.' His voice was sarcastic. He paused. 'I shouldn't have thought he'd be able to tell you any more than Bobby— provided you could trace him, that is, and it wouldn't be easy. I told you—none of that family live here now.'

'I still think it might be worth it,' Isobel said obstinately, stung by his indifference.

'Then by all means try,' he retorted coldly, 'since you're so keen on the idea. Tell me,' his voice became casual, 'do you remember Edmund at all? Did you like him, as your sister did?'

There was now an unmistakable edge in his voice, and Isobel stared at him in surprise, trying to work out what had caused the sudden antagonism. Finally she shook her head.

'No. I don't remember anything about him—liking him, or disliking him.'

'Poor Edmund.' His voice was flat. 'Erased. Dismissed. Nonexistent. I shouldn't bother if I were you. There are other approaches you could take that might be much more profitable.'

He swung the car in through the gates of Stokesay Priory as he said this, his tone lighter, but curiously final. Isobel said nothing. She didn't agree with him, but since the suggestion seemed to annoy him, she would say no more on the matter. Still, she felt a small dart of rebellion. His reaction seemed so illogical. After all, it was he who had advised her to go in search of her past—and she wouldn't allow him to dictate to her how she did it, either, she resolved, as he pulled the car up abruptly at the base of the steps.

'If you'll forgive me,' he turned to her, 'there's some estate business I have to see to—it won't take long. You go on in.'

'All right.' She glanced at him—the matter had not been mentioned before, which seemed odd—but his manner was perfectly normal.

'Would you mind if I tried to telephone Bobby?' She

turned back, her hand still on the door handle. 'I ought
to speak to her, and I tried to get her before we left.'

'Of course.' He smiled up at her, his manner now just
as it had been before, so that Isobel felt relief. 'Call by
all means. I'll be back in under an hour—get Mrs
Deering to make you some tea—you must be cold.'

But Bobby proved impossible to contact. Isobel tried
her stepfather's house first, but Mrs Spencer was
adamant. No, definitely, there had been no call from
Bobby. If there had been she would have given her
Isobel's number in Devon as instructed . . . Yes, yes, if
she called today or tomorrow the message would be
given.

Isobel hung up with a frown. She hesitated, and then
rang the number of Bobby's agency in New York. She
hated doing that, because the agency was a large and
high-powered one, and didn't take kindly to models
being contacted on family grounds. This time their
reaction was just as she had expected: courteous and
impatient. Yes, Miss St Aubyn had flown on to
Barbados; but they weren't shooting the pictures there,
they were moving on to one of the smaller islands. No,
as of now they had no contact number. Yes, of course,
as soon as Miss St Aubyn called in they would give her
the message.

Isobel sighed and hung up. Damn Bobby, she
thought. It was so typical of her—to make a great
drama out of something and then to disappear off the
face of the earth. She felt a momentary alarm, and then
shrugged it aside. She could get Bobby the money.
When she finally deigned to call the news would be
good . . .

She wandered desultorily back and forth in the
sitting-room for a little while, unable to settle or relax,
her mind filling again with the inconclusive events of
the day. A little while later, Mrs Deering brought her a
tray of tea, and home-made scones and jam, and set
them down with a flourish before the fire.

'There you are, my dear. You could do with a good
hot cup of tea, I'll be bound.' She paused, seeming

disposed to linger, and Isobel saw the alert brown eyes move to her face. 'Did you have a nice drive—you and Mr Eliot? Rather a cold day to be up on the moors . . .'

'Yes—yes, it was a little cold,' Isobel answered her absently. She hesitated, but Mrs Deering made no move to leave, and so, gathering her courage, she ventured on.

'This is such a lovely house.' She gestured around the room. 'You've worked here a long time, Mrs Deering, I think Eliot said.'

Mrs Deering's face broadened into a wide smile. 'Why, bless you, my dear. It must be near on forty years now. I came here as a young girl—my first place, it was. Never occurred to me I'd stay. But it suited, and I suited, it seems, and so . . .'

Her voice suddenly trailed away, and Isobel cut in quickly.

'Oh, I didn't realise it was so long! In that case, you might remember my family. We used to live down here, you know. At Aston Deverall. Did Eliot mention that?'

The housekeeper's face took on a closed expression. 'No—I can't say as he did.' She smoothed down her dress. 'Well, I must be getting back to my kitchen, I suppose. There's dinner to be got ready, and . . .'

'You don't remember them? The St Aubyns?' Isobel pressed on.

Mrs Deering shook her head. 'Well no—I'm afraid not. But then we lead a quiet life here. Mr Eliot's uncle was away a lot, and I've never been one to . . .'

'Then maybe you remember some of my friends.' Isobel raised her face and looked directly at her. 'They lived not far from here.' She swallowed, and then forced herself to go on. 'The Delahayes. Their mother was an invalid, and there were two boys—Julius and Edmund.'

A deep flush mounted the housekeeper's neck and face. Her eyes took on a stony expression. 'Delahaye? Delahaye? Can't say as I do. Born and bred in these parts, were they?'

Isobel hesitated. 'Well, I don't know. I think they'd

lived here for some years, certainly. The boys went to boarding school, of course, but . . .'

'Well, now—I might have heard their names mentioned once or twice, years ago. But I can't say as I ever knew them personally. And now, if you'll excuse me, Miss Latimer . . .'

She left the room quickly, before Isobel could say any more. Isobel stared after her, her nerves suddenly prickling and alert. She was lying; of that Isobel did not have a second's doubt. The name had registered, and Mrs Deering was no better at untruths than she herself was. She frowned. Why? Why? Why would she lie to a simple query like that one? Unless . . .

She straightened up in her chair, and stared into the fire, a sudden thought coming to her.

Unless she had been *told* to lie, she thought. And there was only one person who could have given that instruction: Eliot Richardson.

But when Eliot returned, some half an hour later, she quickly dismissed all such thoughts. He burst into the room, his eyes and face alight with excitement and animation, greeting her with a warmth and gentleness that touched her and made her heart race. Quickly he crossed the room to her and held out his hands, drawing her to her feet. One look into his eyes dispelled all suspicion, and Isobel felt ashamed. She was getting jumpy, she thought happily—jumpy and paranoid. It was absurd to have such fancies . . . absurd.

'My darling.' He drew her to him, and his use of that word, the first time he had ever used it, brought the colour instantly to her cheeks, as awareness of him, knowledge and love of him, shot through her body.

He kissed her very gently on the lips, then drew back and looked down into her face. 'We've been fools. Idiots. Something was staring us in the face, and we didn't see it. Just now, it came to me. Now—listen—you remember I told you to bring your passport?'

'Yes.'

'Then go and fetch it, will you? Quickly . . .'

When she returned, Eliot was pacing up and down

the room. The moment she came in, he crossed and took it from her, and began riffling through the pages. Isobel stared at him in bewilderment.

Finally he gave a shout of triumph.

'I knew it. I knew it! Look, Isobel—look there.'

He held out the document to her, and Isobel stared at it blankly. It was open at one of the visa pages.

'My sweet idiot—don't you see? Look!' With one finger he pointed to the page in front of her. 'It's stamped—don't you see? Entry and exit visa stamps. Dated. You arrived in Algeria on December the twenty-second and you left on December the twenty-third. You crossed the border into Morocco—look there's the border post stamp—also December the twenty-third— and you must have travelled to Fez in Morocco, because you flew out of there—look, there's the stamp—on January the sixth. Look at the dates, Isobel, look at the year, you see!' He raised his face to hers, triumph in his eyes. 'It was just before the accident. A matter of *weeks*. You were in Algeria, you crossed straight into Morocco, you stayed there over a week, you flew back—and the accident happened later the same month. *Now* do you see?'

Isobel stared at the page before her blankly. The small triangular black stamps focused, then blurred as her eyes filled with tears. Seeing her reaction, Eliot put his arm around her shoulder and drew her to him.

'My darling—don't be sad—don't be. Don't you see, we're getting somewhere at last? It all begins to add up—the postcard, this, everything. And it must be connected with the accident in some way—it must be, I feel it in my bones. Why else did they all lie to you— why was this never mentioned?' He tilted her face up to him, and looked down into her eyes. 'Think, Isobel. My darling, put two and two together. Shortly before the accident happened, you went to Algeria. From there you sent your stepfather a postcard, telling him you were safe and happy, and not to try and locate you. Within a day—obviously you knew he might check flights, and you were covering your tracks—you crossed the border into Morocco. You stayed there, then you came back. Then there was the accident. Now think. What's the one thing, the most likely thing, that would explain that kind of action?'

Isobel stared at him. Her mouth and throat felt dry.

'You mean I went there with a man? To be with a man? Someone my stepfather didn't want me to be with—so he'd try and stop me if he could? Is that what you think?'

'It's exactly what I think.' His mouth had set grimly. 'In fact I think more than that.' He paused, and his eyes held hers. 'After all who above all among the men you knew then, do we know your stepfather hated and disliked—had banned you and your sister from seeing?'

Isobel gave a low moan of distress. 'It can't be—it isn't possible!'

'I think it is.' Eliot's voice cut across her sharply. 'I think you travelled there in secret, to be with a man your stepfather wouldn't have allowed to cross the threshold. A man you remembered, even after the accident. A man you were in love with . . .' He paused. 'I think you went to Morocco to be with Julius.'

'It's not true!' She wrenched her head away. 'I'd remember—oh, Eliot, if that had happened, surely I'd remember something.'

His arms tightened around her.

'My darling—no, very possibly not. Don't you see, the reason you've blocked it all off is that it isn't arbitrary—it's connected. You went away with a man you loved. You came back—something happened—a quarrel—difficulties with your stepfather—there's an accident, and the next thing you learn is that the man is dead.' He paused, and again gently tilted her face back to his.

'Don't you see, Isobel?' he said tenderly. 'He was your *lover*, and then you found out he was dead. *That* was the shock—*that* was the trauma. That was why you lost your memory.'

Isobel stared up into his face. She could see his eyes, alight with apparent tenderness and concern; she could feel the gentle pressure of his arms. And then his face was becoming shadowed, obscured; it was receding into the dark, and being replaced by another face, a younger face, and the eyes that looked down at her were not dark but a steely grey—except they did not look at her with hatred, as they always had in her dreams, they looked at her with tenderness, and with love.

She swayed, and shut her eyes, pain welling up through her body, and Eliot caught her to him, and rocked her in his arms.

'My darling, we're going to win. I know we are—we're on the right track at last—I sense it, I believe it.'

His voice soothed her. When he felt her body relax against him, he looked down into her face.

'You're not afraid? You want to go on? No matter . . .' He hesitated. 'No matter what we might discover as a result?'

'Yes.' Isobel met his eyes, and he smiled.

'Then let's go and pack.'

'Pack?'

'Of course. We're taking the plane to Morocco in the morning.'

'You're mad—you know that, don't you?'

Isobel settled back in the seat of the plane, and Eliot smiled and pressed her hand. She smiled at him happily.

'When I first met you,' she went on, 'I thought you were—oh, I don't know! Cold, and tight-laced, and cautious. A money man, a banker. And now I find you're none of those things. You're wild, and impulsive and crazily extravagant. I just get used to the idea that one night I'm in Devon, and the next day I'm going to be on a plane to North Africa—and then I discover it's *your* plane.'

'It'll get us there as well as any other.' He sounded amused. 'Only more quickly.'

'But I didn't even know you *had* a plane.'

Eliot smiled with a maddening complacency. 'There's a lot of things you don't know about me.'

'And that's true too.' Isobel looked at him ruefully. 'I know practically nothing about you at all . . .'

'What sort of information had you in mind?'

'Well, I don't know. Your parents, your family. That sort of thing.'

'Nothing much to tell.' His face had sobered, and he pressed her hand a little tighter. 'Isobel—only two events of any great significance have happened in my life. The first I told you about . .'

He paused, and she looked at him curiously.

'And the second?'

'The second happened just recently.' He spoke quite quietly, and without emotion, but Isobel's heart leapt. She glanced up at him shyly, and saw that his eyes had darkened. For a second, just for a second, she saw a trace of the old bitterness, and then it lifted and was gone. 'I thought for a time that what had happened before, had not just scarred me, but crippled me in some way. It had certainly altered my nature—not for the better . . .'

'And now?'

He gave an ironic smile. 'Now I'm not so sure. Let's just say that I hate less than I did. And . . .' He paused, drily. 'That seems to be connected with you in some way.'

'You make me feel happy,' Isobel said simply, and again, just for a second, she saw a darkness in his eyes, there and then gone. He smiled.

'I'm glad. Perhaps that's what it is. Happiness. It's a state of being I'd forgotten had existed . . .'

Isobel swallowed. 'Perhaps you should do as you advised me, one day. Look for your own past.'

'Perhaps.' He shrugged. 'On the whole, though, I think I'd rather leave it where it was—in the past. Just now I'm quite looking forward to the future.'

Again her heart leapt, and her pulse quickened. He had turned from her to the window as he spoke, his voice quite casual. Isobel looked at his harsh profile, at the deep line that ran from nose to chin and emphasised the expressiveness, the sensuality, of his mouth. Oh, please let him mean what I think he means, she prayed silently, and a little wildly. Please . . .

'We're crossing the coastline—look.' He gestured out of the window. 'We'll be landing in a few minutes. I've booked us into the Palace Hotel. It's on the outskirts of the Kasbah—the old Arab city. It's very good, I believe—certainly the most famous of the hotels in Fez, and there aren't that many. If you stayed in an hotel when you were here there's a chance that you stayed there, or at least visited it.' He released her hand. 'It's about half an hour from the airport. I've booked us adjoining rooms.'

Adjoining suites, he might have said, Isobel thought when they arrived. She looked around her in excitement. Her rooms were furnished in the Moroccan style, the floor covered with hand-painted tiles. Low, silk-covered divans flanked an old table of beaten brass, on which the waiter had just placed a tray with a tiny cup, and a long-handled pot filled to the brim with richly scented black coffee. Through an arched stone window she looked out to a courtyard garden; and through another archway lay the bedroom. Isobel slipped off her shoes, and treading on the soft silk and fur of the rugs, padded into that room. It was dominated by the bed—a bed for a harem, she thought. Wide and low, piled with rough silk cushions, it had an extraordinary headboard: old wood, fashioned into Islamic patterns of lilies and ogee arches, it was set with mirror glass. With a smile she threw herself down on it and stretched luxuriously. From above her head the image of her own body was reflected and refracted a hundred times. A bed made for lovemaking, of that she had no doubt; a bed for a thousand and one nights . . . She smiled to herself. It made her feel like Scheherazade.

'It came from one of the old king's palaces in the South.' Eliot's voice cut drily across her thoughts. 'You suit it very well.'

Isobel straightened up abruptly, and Eliot laughed. 'I didn't hear you come in!'

'I knocked. Not very loudly . . .'

She saw his eyes run lazily over her figure, along the slender curve of leg and thigh, up over her breasts to the colour that mounted in her cheeks.

'I think though,' he went on evenly, 'that your Western clothes don't suit it. We'll have to buy you something Moroccan—a kaftan. Diaphanous silk, that sort of thing . . .'

Isobel got up crossly. 'And an embroidered yashmak, I suppose,' she said a little tartly, suspecting him of teasing her. Eliot smiled.

'Oh no.' He shook his head. 'Nothing that hides your face . . .' He touched her cheek lightly as he spoke, and a tremor ran through her body. 'Come and have some coffee. Then we'll make plans.'

When he had poured them both cups of the thick sweet coffee, he sat down on one of the divans, and stretched out his long legs.

'Now,' he looked up at her, 'I've made some enquiries already. This hotel——' He paused. 'Well, it's very famous, and over the years it's housed a number of celebrated guests. They pride themselves on their guest books—Picasso signed his entry with a little sketch— that kind of thing. They were only too delighted to show me some of them. And so we know one thing— either you stayed elsewhere when you were here before, or you stayed here under another name . . .'

'I expect I stayed somewhere else,' Isobel interrupted quickly. 'After all, this hotel must be terribly expensive. I probably stayed in some little *pension* place.'

'I doubt it.' Eliot drained his cup and stood up. 'This isn't Paris or Rome, you know. There are only two other hotels of any size that existed then. Europeans don't often stay in the very small places. Certainly a woman alone . . .'

'But you said—that is—I might not have been alone.'

'Indeed.' His eyes met hers for a second, then glanced away. 'Anyway, it's worth making enquiries at the other two places I mentioned. And then . . .' He shrugged. 'We could walk round the old city—explore the

Kasbah. It's very beautiful. And—who knows? Maybe
something will jog your memory—something quite by
chance. And if it doesn't . . .'

He broke off, his eyes meeting hers once more,
something in his tone bringing the blood rushing to
her cheeks.

'If it doesn't?'

'Then we'll have to try other means, shan't we?' He
smiled into her eyes, and drew her forward by the hand.
'Later.'

Although Eliot had warned her what to expect, Isobel
was still unprepared for the experience of the old city,
for its sudden assault on her mind and senses. From the
hill above, the Kasbah looked still and quiet; its walls
and towers and domes were the soft brown of a faded
rose in the winter sunlight, the same colour as the earth
all around them. But the minute Eliot had steered her
past the crowd of eager boys, each of whom cried out in
English that he was the best, the most trustworthy, the
most efficient of guides, and had led her under the great
archway and into the city, her eyes and her ears and her
nose were besieged with a multitude of sensations.

Immediately they were in a cobbled narrow street,
jostled on all sides by people. Within minutes she was
lost in the labyrinth of tiny winding passageways. Now
they pressed themselves against a wall to let a Berber
tribesman pass, his arms laden with bales of turquoise
silk. Then it was a donkey with laden panniers; then a
group of Moroccan women, clad in black from head to
foot, the loose folds of their head-dresses wound
modestly about their faces, and kept that way, Isobel
noted with a smile, by the simple device of clenching the
material between their teeth.

The smell of the city was strong, almost indescribable:
compounded of people, of animals, of sandalwood
being burned in little braziers, of coffee as they passed
one house, of the clean green scent of mint tea as they
passed another. They rounded another corner, and
found themselves in the market streets. Here were the

metal-workers, and the air rang as they hammered
patterns into brass. Then a street of stalls selling herbs
and spices and dye powders: mounds of cumin and
coriander, heaps of precious saffron, delicately laid out
for display on vine leaves. At the next stall, sticks of
sandalwood, and twenty different shades of henna
powder, the vivid blue of ground indigo. A little girl by
the stall, her beautiful dark eyes outlined with kohl,
lifted her hand and then her bare foot. She was
demonstrating her wares, Isobel realised, for, like most
of the children, her palms and the soles of her feet were
dyed bright orange with henna.

Smiling, Eliot waited by her side as Isobel bought
some sandalwood, and waited while the stall-holder
carefully weighed it in his brass balance, wrapped it in
shiny brown paper and sealed it with vivid wax. Then
he hesitated for a moment, frowning slightly, as if
trying to remember the way, then led her towards a
small, dark shop about halfway along the street. 'Here,
I think. Yes, here . . .'

He stopped, and together they gazed into the interior.
One old man sat there alone, sipping a glass of mint tea.
He sat in a dimly lit Aladdin's cave, full of things so
lovely that Isobel caught her breath. There were silk
hangings, and embroideries like flower gardens. There
were bales of heavy textured silk in all the colours in the
rainbow. There were belts of old leather worked in
gold, antique coats and tunics that a prince or princess
might have worn, lined with fox fur, made of soft
velvet, embroidered with silver and gold thread. There
were cushions and rugs, and, in one corner, a trestle
table draped with black velvet and arranged with
necklaces and belts and bracelets and rings, of silver
and turquoise and coral and lapis lazuli.

'Come with me.'

What happened next was like a dream. Eliot led them
into the shop, and the old man rose and bowed to them
courteously. Isobel was seated; the old man clapped
his hands, a young boy brought her a glass of mint
tea. Then, while she watched, bemused, Eliot and the

shop-keeper embarked on protracted negotiations. Now
in English, now Arabic, now French. Bales of silk were
brought down; Eliot shook his head. The old man
raised his eyes to the heavens and protested volubly,
though Isobel thought that secretly he was both amused
and pleased.

'You have judgment, *monsieur*. Now—we shall be
serious, yes? We will not waste time with trifles . . . *avec
les choses pour les touristes . . .*'

Silently, Isobel sipped the cool sweet tea and
watched. Colours fluttered before her eyes: saffron
yellow; a green as pale as the stalks of young bulbs;
Imperial purple; shocking pink; indigo blue; beige,
grey, cream, white. She shut her eyes, lulled by the
old man's voice and tired after the flight and their
long walk. It was warm in the little shop, and
shadowy; somewhere she could smell sandalwood
burning . . .

'Lapis . . .' She heard Eliot's voice, dreamily, as if
from a distance, and at once her mind snapped, became
alert. *I have been here before.* From nowhere the
thought sprang into her mind. Her eyes opened. She
stared across the little shop. Eliot was bending over one
of the tables, his body clearly outlined against the light.
She saw his shape only, the classic line of his profile, the
wide shoulders, the arm reaching forward. *With Julius*,
her mind said. *With Julius.*

She straightened; for a second she felt her mind
grapple, then lose its grip on the memory, like trying to
grasp a dream on waking and feeling it slip away.
Perhaps she drew in her breath; certainly something
made Eliot look up at her abruptly.

'Isobel—are you all right?'

'I'm fine—fine.' Her voice sounded quite normal. The
memory was gone as suddenly as it came. She felt sweat
bead her brow, a sensation of dizziness, and then
composure again.

A short while afterwards the old man bowed them
courteously from the shop. Eliot's arms were full of
packages; he turned to her, his eyes meeting hers. 'You

remembered?' It was hardly a question. 'Something happened? Then? In that shop?'

Isobel nodded tiredly, and told him. His mouth tightened.

'You're tired. You look very pale. Come on, I'll take you back to the hotel. We can have something to eat, and then you should rest . . .'

He led her forward, holding her arm, his grip tight. He stopped just once on the way back.

'You're sure that was all?' He looked down at her, his eyes dark and watchful. 'Nothing more? You thought of him . . .' He seemed reluctant to pronounce Julius's name. 'And then it was gone? No image? No association?'

'No, nothing. Just that,' Isobel answered flatly.

Eliot swore, and then quickened their pace.

'You have eyes the colour of lapis lazuli—you see? This dark blue, with little flecks of gold—and so I bought you this.' He smiled, and laid a package gently on the bed beside her.

'And you have hair like silk, so I bought you this . . .' He laid another package beside her.

'You have a tiny waist—so this seemed appropriate . . .' Another small parcel was carefully placed beside her. He paused. One last small box lay in the palm of his hand.

'And this . . . I don't know why I bought this. No good reason, except I liked it.' He paused, looking down at her, then smiled. 'It's late. You've been asleep a long while. Look—Isobel—it's night.'

She raised her eyes to his face, then turned to the window. Outside the sky was black, and spread with stars.

'So, I've waited patiently. Now I'd like you to open them—and then, even more, I'd like you to wear them. For me.'

Isobel slowly raised her eyes to his face. Her lids felt heavy, she still had not shaken off her sleep and a dream she could not recall but which had left behind it a glow of remembered pleasure, of a secret stealing warmth. 'You kissed me,' she said slowly, in mock accusation. 'You kissed me awake, I'm almost sure of it.'

'I might have done. I may do so again.' His mouth lifted mockingly and Isobel's pulse raced suddenly faster. 'But just now, open the parcels.'

Isobel sat up, shaking her tousled hair back from her face. She lifted the first of the packages, then looked up at him, her cheeks flushed. 'It's so exciting—like Christmas! Thank you, Eliot.'

'Open them.'

With trembling fingers she undid them one by one, carefully smoothing back the soft tissue paper. When they were all open except the one he still held in the palm of his hand, she lifted her eyes shyly to his in delight. 'Eliot, they're beautiful. So beautiful ... I've never ... no one has ever ...'

He interrupted her quickly, and lifted the heavy necklace of lapis and silver. 'This is to rival your eyes ... there.' He fastened it around her throat. 'You begin to look pagan already. This ...' He lifted the old leather belt exquisitely worked with silver flowers. 'This is to fasten round your waist. But you have to put this on first. Then I'll fasten it for you.'

He lifted the pale tumble of fine silk that was spread out across her lap: a dress, cut with deceptive simplicity, like a plain tunic. The silk was fine, so fine that as Isobel lifted it reverently over her hand she saw her own skin glow through it. Spread out in the light it was the colour of milk; gathered into heavy folds it was the colour of honey.

'It's a wedding tunic. An Arab woman would wear it next to her skin, and over it, of course, she'd wear a lot of other things, bodices and skirts and over-skirts and veils ...' He paused, his voice dry. 'However, as an emancipated Western woman, and here alone with me in this room, I don't see why you shouldn't wear it just as it is—do you?'

He lifted his face as he spoke, and his eyes met hers.

Isobel looked at him silently. She knew the unspoken
implication in his words; she knew what must, almost
inevitably, happen, if she put this on now, and she
sensed he was, in his way, warning her of that. There
was a moment's silence; the room shadowed, then grew
bright, then shadowed again. She felt a sensation of
time standing still, of time spinning, a second that was
like a spell, as if Eliot's dry words were a secret
incantation. Then, slowly, she stood up. 'Close your
eyes.'

He did as he was bid. She hesitated a moment, her
hands trembling, and then quickly she took off her
Western clothes, her Western underclothes. She stood
for a moment feeling the air suddenly cool against her
bare skin and looked out at the stars. Then she reached
across, and slipped the tunic over her head. It fell in
soft folds from throat to ankle, like finest gossamer.
Through it, she saw, glancing down, her body was at
first revealed—its shadows, its planes, the curves of her
hips, the thrust of her pale breasts—and then, as she
moved, obscured again and hidden. The ritual pleased
her.

'Open your eyes,' she said softly, and Eliot did so.

He looked at her in silence, then slowly he stood up.
He looked down into her face steadily, and then,
quietly, he said her name. She knew it was a question;
she bent her head. Eliot sighed, stepped forward,
gathered her in his arms and bent his mouth to her lips.

He kissed her, gently at first, his hands moving up to
span her waist and draw her body against him, his
tongue tracing the soft full outline of her lips. Isobel
trembled; she felt her body tense, then relax against
him as the moist sweet warmth beat up like a great
wave through her body. She sighed against his mouth;
his breath caught, and instantly, hungrily, he deepened
his kiss, parting her lips fiercely to the thrust of his
tongue, so that her mouth felt possessed by his.

Pressed close against him, naked under the thin silk,
she felt his body harden and pulse against her belly, and
answering fire shot through her blood, arcing through

her so that she clung to him in a sudden desperation of
passion, an urgency of desire so intense that all thought
was blotted out. She knew nothing but his touch, the
moist sweetness of his mouth, the hardness of his body,
the raggedness of their breathing.

He lowered his mouth to her throat, and she arched it
back, inviting his kisses that sought the hectic pulse and
made her cry out, a little animal cry of longing. Quickly
his hands moved up, unfastened the necklace and tossed
it aside. They slipped down, glancingly, over the hollow
at the base of her throat, over the jut of her breasts.
Isobel shuddered, and his grip tightened. She felt her
breasts swell under his touch, felt the wide aureole of
her nipples harden and engorge with blood as, lightly,
tantalisingly, he touched them through the silk and
then, as if losing control, maddened by the thin fabric
which covered her nakedness, thrust it aside and cupped
the weight of her breasts to his mouth and tongue. He
drew the hard nipples into his mouth, first one, then the
other, and Isobel arched back, pressing her hips and
thighs against his aroused hardness, lifting her breasts
with a fierce gladness to the caress of his lips.

He drew back then, just a little, and looked down
into her face, his eyes dark, questioning, as if for a
second he still doubted her, still thought she might draw
back. When, impulsively, she moved to him, he gave a
low groan. 'Let me see you. Let me look at you . . .'

With one quick movement the single fastening was
undone, the silk swept aside. He paused, his eyes falling
to her body, to the slender pallor of her skin, the arched
breasts, their points hard and rosy from his kisses, the
gentle curve of stomach and hips, the tiny triangle of
dark hair. His hand tightened on the silk; he tossed it
aside, with one quick angry movement, and she stood
naked before him. She reached for him then, and he
caught her hand, pressing it against him so that his flesh
leapt and grew at her touch. Then, gently, he gathered
her against him, held her a moment tenderly, then lifted
her and laid her back against the silk cushions of the
bed. Isobel lay back and looked at him.

She felt no shyness, only consuming desire that mixed and married with the love she felt for him. Want and love beat through her body; her blood pulsed with urgency and impatience. He reached for the fastenings of his shirt, his tie, his belt, ripping at them in his impatience. And then he stood before her, the light catching the strong golden planes of his body, shadowing the dark hair on chest and loins, glittering, catching and refracting in the tiny panes of mirror glass behind her. Quickly he bent, moved beside her, drew her body with one swift passionate movement against the length of his, as if he could wait no longer; as if, like her, he had moved beyond all rationality to a new darker animal place of breathing, touching, wanting. She cried out at the touch of his bare skin against hers, cried out with longing, and instinctively her hands reached for him. But he caught them tight in his, and held her, and looked down into her face. She saw the want there, the intentness and concentration of desire in his eyes, and she saw the effort it cost him to hold back, just for this moment.

'Wait,' he said roughly. 'Dear God, wait. I have to know. Tell me . . .' His voice caught and broke.

Her breathing steadied, she looked deep into his eyes. Then, very deliberately, she released her hands from his and moved them down over his body. Over the strong hard muscles of shoulders and chest; over the long curve of his spine; over the hard narrow bones of the pelvis, and down to where his flesh moved, quick to her soft touch. She cried out then, incoherently, wonderingly, and as he groaned, she said his name, gently at first, little more than a whisper, then again and again, drawing him down to her mouth, willing him, telling him, that she wanted this, that she wanted him, that now no ghost from the past could come between them.

He believed her; the quick urgent triumph as his mouth came down on hers told her that. He moved, straddling her, catching her body and lifting it up to him between the hardness of his thighs, hair against hair, skin against skin, softness against strength, so a

moist sweetness flowered in her blood, beat up through
her body, demanded his touch. Her lips were parted,
her tongue drawn into his mouth, the whole of her
womb felt open to him, and she longed for him to touch
her there, there where she most longed for his touch
and his thrust. Feverishly, their bodies moving against
one another, she tried to part her thighs to the caresses
she ached for. But he held her, and made her wait,
made her be slow, made her keep pace with him. She
heard, as if from far away, the quick pant of their
breathing, the thud of his heart as she lifted her head
and pressed it against the hair of his chest.

He groaned then, and his own hands moved down, as
if he could not, would not, wait any longer. With a low
sigh he parted her thighs, his fingers caressing the soft
secret skin on the inside of her thighs, parting her,
stroking the soft moist crevices of her flesh.

'Yes—ah yes . . .' She cried out, and he lifted her to
him, arching her body up. She felt his touch, shut her
eyes, slipped back into a black place of desire, where
she had no being but this. His hands sought her breasts,
and crushed them with a violence that heightened the
wildness of desire she felt mounting in her. She opened
her eyes then, terrified and aroused by this combination
of fierceness, languor and powerful control. She looked
up at him, at his body strong and powerful above hers,
and as she met his eyes, saw the effort this control cost
him, she felt a new savage sexual rhythm start to beat
through nerves and blood and pulse against him in the
depths of her womb.

She moved under him; she moved with him; he thrust
deeper and faster, then held back, then as she clutched
at him in a wild desperation, sank deeper again. She
knew this rhythm, she thought; she knew it and she
exulted in it. With new urgency she drew him down, so
his hands held her breasts, and his mouth was on hers.
Her hands moved down, over his back, feeling the
tension and clench of his muscles, the voluptuous
strength and smoothness of his skin.

Sweat bathed their skin; their bodies moved together;

their breath came faster; he pushed her back, taking his weight on his hands on either side of her body, and she lifted herself to him, so the hard nipples of her breasts rubbed against the dark damp hair of his chest. He groaned then, and she cried out for release. At her cry his movements changed, became fiercer, harder, more demanding. He moved his mouth then, and said her name, said other things that heightened and quickened her arousal, so she clung to him, and up out of the dark, she felt her body sweep with its own tide, a mounting tide that swept her up and on to some edge, some chasm, some remembered place which burned with a black fire.

'Yes,' he said, 'yes.' And as she felt his body jerk within her, shudder against her, her body went with him, kept time, and went over into the fire.

I love you, Eliot, she said silently. *I love you.* And she wound her arms around him, and held him tight against her heart.

CHAPTER SEVEN

THEY slept then. Later he made love to her again, and then again, as night moved into morning, as if nothing could satiate the knowledge and desire that had quickened between them. At last, when the light of day striped the room through the shutters, Isobel slipped from his embrace and from between the sheets. She stood at the end of the wide bed and looked down at him as he slpet, her heart filled with a great tenderness and contentment.

Eliot lay stretched out, his black hair tousled, and still damp from their love-making. One strong arm was thrown back against the pillow; one sheet, drawn over them in the long night, clung to the long line of hips and thighs. Isobel stood still, looking at him, and her heart contracted.

The doctor was wrong, she thought, quite wrong. Nothing had come back from the past, no hint nor shadow of it. And now she felt gloriously free, free as she had not felt for five years, as if the past were dead and gone and never to return to her. She wondered now that she had cared about those lost years; she did not care for them now. They could vanish—had vanished. If her memory of them never came back she felt now as if she did not care. This was the memory that would matter to her: this night and this place and this man and what had happened between them. The present— she cared for that. And the future too, she thought, and Eliot stirred.

He opened his eyes and looked up at her, instantly alert. There was a silence, a steadiness between them, held in that long look. It was as if he were waiting for something, Isobel thought, waiting for her to say something quite calmly, quite patiently, as if there were no possible doubt as to what she might say. When she

118

did not speak, he slowly lifted his hand from the bed
and held it out to her. She ran to him and he drew her
down beside him, and under the sheet, wrapping his
arms and thighs around hers with a gentle familiarity, a
shared knowledge that lit the happiness that burned in
her heart. She turned her face to his on the pillow, and
looked into his eyes.

'I love you, Eliot,' she said quietly, and she felt his
clasp tighten against her.

'Do you?' he said slowly. 'Do you?'

For answer she pressed her face against his neck, and
he held her gently against him. Again she thought he
waited; attuned now to his body she could feel the
tension in it, though his clasp remained gentle, his limbs
relaxed. But he said nothing, and eventually he sighed
and straightened up, drawing her with him. He smiled,
and reached out to the table beside him, his hands
seeking the fourth package, the one he still had not
given her and which had been forgotten the night
before.

'Here. I wanted you to have this.'

He held it out to her, and she thought his hand
trembled slightly. She looked up at him, but his eyes
told her nothing; he met her questioning gaze evenly,
his eyes dark, his expression unreadable. Slowly,
hesitantly, she unwrapped the paper and opened the
small leather box.

Eliot moved then, quickly, and took it from her
before she could speak. He pushed back the lid, and
took out the ring inside. Isobel stared at it as it lay in
the palm of his hand. It was a simple circle of gold, like
a wedding ring. He lifted it so she could look at it
closely, and she saw that though the outside was plain,
the inside was engraved. She stared at it uncertainly,
then looked more closely. It was not a date, not a name;
instead it was a design, intricately worked: the initial 'I',
repeated twice, the two letters bound together.

'My initial?' She lifted her eyes to his. He met her
gaze steadily.

'An "I"—yes.' He smiled, his mouth twisting a little

at the corners, as if there were some irony she were missing, and her blindness pained him.

'Repeated twice?'

'So it seems.' Again he smiled. Then he took her hand, her right hand, and slipped it on the ring finger. 'Too tight.' He shrugged. 'We'd better try the other hand.'

Slowly he lifted her left hand, holding it for a moment in his. Then, very gently, he removed the ring, and slipped it on to the third finger. It fitted perfectly. His hand closed over hers. Their eyes met, Isobel's wide with uncertainty, seeing that he attached great significance to this, but unsure, afraid to be sure, of what it meant for him.

As if he read her thoughts, he lifted her hand and kissed it. 'Our ring,' he said, and there was a catch in his voice. 'It means whatever you want it to mean. But I thought . . .' He paused, as if about to say one thing, and then deciding to say another. 'I thought we should mark the—bond—between us.'

'The bond?'

'This bond,' he said, a little grimly, and, reaching down with a swiftness that took her by surprise, and taking her hand, pulled it roughly against him, so that hand and ring were pressed against the sudden hardening of his flesh. The imperiousness of the gesture, its frankness, the flash of something like anger dark in his eyes as if he dared her to deny what he felt, what she felt, all this quickened in her body, so fire shot up from her womb.

She sighed. He pushed her back roughly and straddled her in one easy movement. Then, poised above her, his hands tightened in her long hair, forced her face to look up at his.

'Look at me,' he said roughly. 'Look at me. Don't shut your eyes. Don't turn your head. Look at me. I want to see you—see your face. When I do this. And *this*——'

Isobel arched involuntarily, and cried out with a swift angry pleasure; heat swept up beneath the skin; he thrust again, and her eyes flickered shut in an ecstasy of response.

'Open them,' he demanded angrily. 'Open them, look at me. Now. And now. And now . . .'

She opened her eyes. She thought he expected to see alienation in her face, or anger—she knew that certainly he was waiting for some response, for it was as if he intended to force it out of her with each withdrawal, each thrust. But quickly she was blinded to that; her body took over. It answered his, and answered it in kind, with a violence and a quickness that matched his. She felt her hands tighten against the muscles of his shoulders, her nails dig into his flesh; she lifted her body up, meeting his gaze boldly, each thrust of him registering, she knew, in the depths of her eyes as well as the depths of her body. Her hips ground against his in a sudden quick savage rhythm; she saw his eyes widen in surprise, his brows contract, and then his face close in the same intensity and desperation of desire she felt.

'You look at *me*,' she said, her voice hardly recognisable to her own ears, as his eyes flickered and half-closed. 'You look at *me*. I want you to know too— what I feel. What I . . . oh God, when you . . .'

He cried out then, and they came together in a sudden quick beating extremity of want. As their bodies trembled, then relaxed, he caught her to him with passionate gentleness, and held her tight in his arms. Then, slowly and lingeringly, he kissed her parted mouth.

He drew her hand down, slipping a little to one side, pulling her hand so it was trapped in the warmth between their bodies. Then he drew her hand up, and kissed her damp palm, kissed the ring on her finger, his eyes never once leaving hers.

'Tell me you won't forget,' he said, his voice harsh with a desperation she had never heard in it. 'Tell me you won't—that you cannot—any more than I can.'

She clasped him to her, passionately, her heart beating with the love she felt for him, and he buried his face against her neck. But not before Isobel glimpsed, though he moved quickly, the angry tears that glittered in his eyes.

The days after that seemed to Isobel like an eternity of happiness in which time no longer obeyed its usual rules but sometimes sped past, and sometimes slowed and stopped so that there were moments when she was with Eliot that she knew she would never forget—no matter what happened.

It was not so much the places they visited she would remember, she thought—beautiful and strange though they were. They visited shops and restaurants; one day they drove out into the desert south of Fez, where the mountains were blue on the horizon, still snow-capped. Another day they feasted on *cous-cous*; another day they drove to the coast and sat in the winter sun looking out over the waters of the Mediterranean. They saw one day an Arab wedding; another day, a funeral, and listened, in silence, their hands clasped, to the strange keening whoops with which the Arab women expressed both ritual joy and ritual mourning. They danced, one night, by candlelight; another night lay before a fire in Isobel's room and talked into the early hours of the morning.

Each of these events she remembered and held to herself, but her recollection of them was disjointed by happiness. She could not have said certainly in what order they occurred, or which day, but they were all alight, lit by the joy she felt in Eliot's company, a joy that radiated and stained the memories so they were golden in recollection. His gravity, his detachment, his wit, his unpredictability—these, as she came to know him better, she loved more and more.

He never said that he loved her, but it did not matter to her. She felt his love, she told herself, every time he touched her. And she wore the ring he gave her. Even when she washed or bathed, she never took it off. It felt magical, like a talisman.

'I feel,' she said to him once, lacing her arms around

his neck, and looking steadily into his eyes, 'I feel as if my past had gone away. I don't care about it any more. I don't care if I never find it. I didn't think that would ever happen.'

Eliot frowned. 'When we go back to England,' he began slowly, 'and we'll have to go back soon, you do realise that, my darling?' He paused. 'You may not feel like that then.'

'I shall,' Isobel replied simply, and Eliot smiled at her certainty. He said nothing, but he kissed her.

They decided, finally, that they would leave on the Saturday. On the Friday Eliot left her alone for a while—not for long, he promised her as he left. Just long enough for him to make the arrangements for the journey. When he had gone, as she had told him she must, Isobel telephoned England and, after some delays, got through at last to her stepfather's home, and to his housekeeper. But the call was inconclusive: Bobby had telephoned twice during her absence, and had been annoyed, Mrs Spencer said, to find that Isobel had gone away.

'I told her, like you said, Miss St Aubyn. Everything was all right, and you'd sorted it out, and she had no cause for worry . . .'

'You're sure you said that?'

'Of course I am! Not as it did much good. She wanted a number to call you, she said, and when I said as how I hadn't got one, she got into one of her tempers. Rung off. I said you'd ring her just as soon as you got back, but she said that was no good, she was moving on again and she'd have to ring herself. Sunday. She said she'd ring Sunday.'

'Oh well, that's all right then.' Isobel heaved a sigh of relief. 'I'm coming back tomorrow, Mrs Spencer. I'll be at the Devon address by Saturday afternoon, and I'll call you then.'

She replaced the receiver, feeling a momentary stab of guilt, which she quickly forced aside. After all, it wasn't entirely her fault. She'd been trying to get Bobby for days before she left, and anyway the matter was settled. Meanwhile she was here and she was with Eliot, and she did have her own life to live, she thought defensively.

She sat for a little while after that in the tiny garden outside her room, leaning back in the shelter of its walls and allowing the winter sunshine to warm her. The sunlight caught the gold of the ring on her finger, and Isobel turned it thoughtfully back and forth, her mind far away, lost in thoughts of Eliot. It was strange, that ring, she thought. Eliot had said no more about it, though he had seemed glad she wore it always. Yet now she had time to be alone and consider, she knew there were many questions she would have liked to have asked.

Had he bought it here in Fez, for instance, with the other things? It was possible, but she doubted it. The local jewellery was all of silver—they had seen virtually no gold in any of the shops. And the ring was Western, not Arabic in design. Had he bought it in England, before they left? That thought touched her, and she smiled to herself, fingering the narrow band of gold.

And the two initials, two entwined letters—that was strange too. She took the ring off and looked at its engraving more closely, wondering if she had been mistaken. But no, there was no doubt. Two letters, both 'I', linked together . . .

A breeze blew across the courtyard, and she shivered. Quickly she put the ring back on her finger and looked at her watch, feeling suddenly restless and on edge. It was past twelve; Eliot had left more than an hour before. She missed him, but more than that, she found the calmness of the past days slipping away from her now that she was alone and had time to think. The reality of their return to England bore in on her suddenly. What would happen then? Where would she go? Where would she live? What would she do about finding work? And what would happen between Eliot and herself once this idyll was over?

Anxious to distract herself and occupy her mind, she left her room and went out into the main body of the hotel. There were shops there, and a newspaper stall that sold English magazines, and a lounge. She would buy a paper and order some coffee, she decided, and wait for Eliot there.

But she was frustrated in her purpose. The hotel was quiet—most of the guests were out, she guessed, and she had only just entered the foyer when the manager greeted her.

He was a young man, and he ran his hotel with great efficiency. Isobel suspected that the romance between herself and Eliot was the subject of considerable speculation among the staff—it would be surprising if it weren't in the circumstances. Now the manager greeted her with a low bow, and told her he was very sad to hear she would be leaving the next day. She would come back, he hoped, she and Mr Richardson, of course—he hoped that their stay had been a very happy one?

Isobel smiled; very happy, she assured him. The manager appeared delighted. Without further prompting, he was launched: the history of the hotel, of the building, of Fez, of his own involvement here. Isobel listened with interest, and the manager drew her to one side.

'Of course, we have had many celebrated guests here,' he was saying proudly. 'In 1929, Picasso, for instance. And Hemingway. Jean Cocteau, you know, the French writer and artist . . .' He raised his eyes and gave a little click of the tongue, as if Cocteau were a celebrity he could not entirely endorse. 'You have not looked at our guest-books, I think? You would like to do so? I should be honoured to show you.'

Isobel hesitated, but there was still no sign of Eliot, and the manager was clearly so genuinely proud and anxious to show her the registers that she smiled and agreed. He drew her into his office with great ceremony, ordered her coffee, and began to lay before her a series of leather-bound ledgers. With gathering interest, Isobel looked through them; the volume from the 'twenties, with the Picasso sketch; a jump forward to the 'forties, back to the 'thirties, on to the late 'sixties, when there had been a flurry of pop stars ... Eventually she looked up, hesitating, yet drawn by a sudden idea. Trying to make her voice casual, she asked if she might look at some of the more recent volumes; she mentioned a date, five years before.

The manager beamed: nothing could be simpler. Within seconds another leather volume lay beside her.

The telephone rang, and the manager expressed his apologies. Some slight problem in the kitchens; if she would excuse him for a few minutes, Mademoiselle had everything she required? Isobel nodded absent-mindedly, and the man left the room.

She stared at the book in silence for a moment, half unwilling to open it. After all, Eliot had already looked through this volume, and she had decided the past was behind her ... and yet she felt curious, tempted.

Her hands trembling a little, she opened the book. July. August. She riffled the pages further. Ah, here it was, December, five years ago. Impatiently she flicked past the entries for the early days of the month, and turned to the Christmas period. December 23rd, that was the date on the passport. Nothing that day; she ran her finger down a column of names. There seemed to have been some convention going on, most of the guests were French, she was wasting her time: no Latimer, no St Aubyn, Eliot was right ...

Suddenly her finger stopped as it ran down the column of names. She felt her skin grow ice-cold. A small gasp broke from her lips, and the page blurred. She shut her eyes and opened them again. The entry was still there, she had not imagined it, and she couldn't conceive how Eliot could have missed it.

December 24th, five years before, *Mr and Mrs E. Delahaye*. No address, simply the word 'England' scrawled in black ink, as if impatiently. Not her handwriting.

She stared at the page, her heart beating wildly in her chest, her mouth suddenly dry. The coincidence was too great for there to be any doubt, surely. She had stayed here then, she *had*. And not alone. She had been masquerading as someone's wife—as *Edmund's* wife.

She stared at the page in wild disbelief. Edmund? It was impossible, impossible. But no, there could be no mistake. The initial was clearly written. There was no way it could be construed as 'J'. Shaking, she leaned back in the chair and shut her eyes, her mind reeling.

Edmund? Edmund? The *other* brother? But she remembered nothing about him, nothing at all. Bobby had said she preferred him to his brother, that he had a nicer nature . . . that was all she knew of him. Her mind rebelled, and she almost cried out in despair. It couldn't be, it was impossible! It was Julius she remembered, Julius who was dead, Julius who had haunted her dreams; Julius, not Edmund.

She kept her eyes tightly closed, and through the swirling confusion of her thoughts the full implication of what she had discovered bore in on her. She *had* come to Morocco; she *had* had an affair; Edmund had been her lover, not his brother—*and Edmund was still alive*.

She drew in her breath sharply and opened her eyes to stare down at the page. Very deliberately she forced herself to sit still, to lay her hands flat on the table, and to steady herself. As she did so, calm gradually returned. Eliot's ring glittered on her finger. Slowly and carefully she shut the ledger.

It was past and it should stay in the past, she thought, setting her mouth tight. Whatever had happened, it was over and gone. Edmund Delahaye was a wraith, a ghost; he meant nothing to her. If he were alive she had no wish to see him, no wish to contact him. After all, he had never contacted her. And if Eliot had found this entry, and she could not doubt, knowing his efficiency, that he had—well, Eliot had obviously decided it was better for her not to know of it, and Eliot was right.

She stood up, feeling a sudden new confidence. She would say nothing to him, she decided. She would forget this had ever happened, and trust her own instincts as she had done the past week. She would think of the present and the future, and be happy with the man she loved.

Quickly and carefully she replaced the ledger on the shelf with the others, walked out of the room, and closed the door. That was it, she thought; the end, the last laying of the ghosts. She walked out of the hotel with a new spring in her step, and waited in the clear sunshine. In the distance the voice of the *muezzin* called the faithful to prayer. The air shimmered above the walls of the old city.

She felt calm and at peace. Fifteen minutes later, Eliot returned, and she ran to meet him.

'Were you sad to leave?'

'Yes.'

'Don't be. We'll go back there one day.' Eliot turned to her with a smile that lit her heart, and gently pressed her hand. The plane banked and tilted; below them Isobel saw the patchwork of ploughed fields, the grey outline of the moor.

'If you wish it, that is.' His grip tightened, and Isobel pressed his hand in return.

'I do wish it.'

His mouth twisted wryly. 'Meanwhile England and the winter once more. There's been a thaw—that's something, I suppose. So.' He paused and met her eyes, his own warm and teasing. 'Meanwhile, we'll go straight back to the Priory. And tonight, after dinner, we'll sit by the fire and we'll burn some of those sticks of sandalwood you insisted on bringing back, just to remind ourselves of Morocco... And we'll talk. And make plans ...'

'And then?' Isobel glanced up at him.

'And then I shall take you to bed. And make love to you thoroughly and at length, just as I did every night—and most days—in Morocco.' He paused, his mouth tightening slightly. 'Some things don't change ...'

Isobel looked up at him curiously, caught by

something odd in his tone. 'Do you believe that, Eliot?' she said quietly.

He met her eyes once more, his own serious, his mouth grave.

'Yes, I do,' he said steadily. 'I believe it of us—and that's all that matters just now.'

He glanced away then, as if this statement were too much, an indulgence he already regretted, and Isobel smiled to herself. It was the nearest he had ever come, this strange, reserved, unpredictable man, to any declaration of his feelings, and it made her heart leap and rejoice far more than any flowery sentiments would have done.

I love him, she thought. I love him—and tonight I shall tell him. Tell him properly. Not when we're making love, but when we are just together. I shall tell him what he means to me—how he has changed my life.

'We'll be landing in a moment.' Eliot turned to her, and Isobel reached across to the seat where she had left her coat. Eliot caught her hand with a smile.

'Leave it,' he said mysteriously. 'You won't be needing it.'

She didn't understand him until they were out on the tarmac, and he opened the door of the familiar black BMW.

'Here.' He reached inside it, and drew out something that had been casually tossed over one of the seats. Isobel stared in disbelief. It was a coat made of fur, long thick soft brown fur—the most beautiful coat she had ever seen. Eliot smiled as he saw her expression.

'You like it?' His voice was quite casual. 'It's sable, so it ought to be warm.'

'Eliot—don't be ridiculous—I can't . . .'

'I don't intend to start arguing on the tarmac,' he interrupted brusquely. 'Now, put it on, woman, before you freeze. I ordered it by Telex from Morocco, so it's probably the wrong size anyway.'

He gripped her by the arms and eased the coat on. It fitted exactly, as if it had been made for her—just as he had known it would, Isobel thought, looking up at him and then laughing with sheer excitement and pleasure. It fell from throat to mid-calf, the softest, warmest fur imaginable. Isobel stroked it for a second, wonderingly, and Eliot looked her up and down composedly.

'Well, I said I thought you looked like a Russian princess before—I just thought we'd better complete the image, that's all.' His manner was quite casual, but Isobel saw that sudden focusing of the eyes, that darkening, that she knew signified his admiration and desire. Instantly she felt the arc of response surge through her own blood, knew the colour mounted in her cheeks. In an instant, though she was not conscious of taking a step, she was in his arms, pressed close against his chest, her mouth seeking his.

His mouth came down on hers, hard and demandingly. It was a long kiss, and it was Eliot who broke it off, cutting through her attempt at muddled protest.

'No arguments—get in the car. And don't look at me like that either, otherwise I shall throw you down on the runway and take you without further ceremony, and that would probably be a bad thing for our health and our reputations.' He pushed her unceremoniously into the front seat. 'Now,' he said, as he slid in beside her, and the powerful engine revved. 'Let's go home, my darling, shall we?'

Eliot drove fast and expertly along the winding roads, concentrating his attention on his driving, his manner slightly impatient and preoccupied, as if he were deep in thought and anxious only to get them home. Isobel was content to sit in silence, her gloved hands laced in the thick fur that lay across her lap. She felt wrapped in warmth, wrapped in happiness.

The light was fading; the tyres hissed on the road. Isobel leaned back on the seat. The moor was to their right now, and on the skyline a single bird was rising, hovering. A hawk of some kind, she thought, narrowing her eyes to look at it. A hawk, or possibly a falcon. She held it in her view for a few moments, black against the last of the light. Then it was gone. She sighed and closed her eyes, feeling for the first time since they had landed a dart of apprehension, an odd touch of melancholy.

Perhaps she slept for a little while, or half-dreamed; anyway, it took her by surprise when she felt the car brake abruptly with a clatter of gravel, and she heard Eliot give a low muttered exclamation. She opened her eyes, and peered out into the gathering darkness. They had reached the Priory; Eliot had pulled up sharply at the foot of the house steps. And there, clear in the headlights, was another car, a flashy car, Isobel thought, seeing Eliot stare at it and frown. The latest registration, with an exaggerated fast-back, spoilers front and rear—the whole vehicle sprayed a lurid metallic gold.

'Guests?' she turned to Eliot enquiringly.

'Not a car I recognise.' His voice was curt. Clearly this manifestation was unexpected and annoying to him. He glared at the car, and then shrugged.

'Well, it can't be anything important. Someone to see Mrs Deering perhaps. . . . Nothing we need bother about.'

Slowly Isobel climbed out of the BMW and began to walk across the drive to the steps. She glanced at the car as she passed it; it had been parked carelessly. On the back seat was a jumble of gear—shiny metal suitcases, wires, something that looked like a huge silver umbrella, and some chrome stands and lamps. She frowned; Eliot strode over to the car, and peered into it, his face scowling. He looked as if he'd like to kick it.

'Photographic equipment . . . what the hell?'

Isobel suddenly froze. She stood stock still, apprehension sweeping up through her body in waves. In that moment, as Eliot still stared at the car in annoyance, the hall light came on, illuminating the drive, the door was thrown back, and Mrs Deering appeared at the top of the steps. It was obvious at once from her manner that something was wrong. She looked perplexed and worried, her hands nervously smoothing down the neat folds of her skirt. She started forward.

'Oh, it's you, Mr Eliot . . . I heard the car, and of course, I was expecting you both, but the thing is . . .'

Eliot turned, his face haughty and tight with anger. 'Who the hell does this car belong to? Has someone turned up? Whoever they are, get rid of them, would you, Mrs Deering? I told you on the telephone—Miss Latimer and I have had a long journey, we're tired, and the last thing we want is . . .'

'I know, Mr Eliot, I know.' The housekeeper glanced over her shoulder and advanced nervously to the top of the steps. 'I told the gentleman that, but he wouldn't listen. Wouldn't take no for an answer. I couldn't get rid of him. He said he'd sit here in the car all night if necessary—and so in the end, I thought I'd better let him in.' She paused. 'Him being a friend of Miss Latimer's and everything . . .'

There was a silence. Isobel felt a cold shiver go down her back. The housekeeper's eyes met hers nervously, and then flicked away. Eliot's face darkened. He took a step forward. 'A friend of Miss Latimer's? That's impossible. . . Where the hell is he? I'll get rid of him then . . .'

He moved to the steps, and as Mrs Deering began to protest once more, suddenly stopped, and slowly turned to Isobel.

'It *is* impossible, I take it?' His voice was now as cold as ice. 'I assume you haven't invited any—friends—to my house?'

Colour flared in Isobel's cheeks, and she swallowed. 'Of course not—no. But . . .' She hesitated, and Eliot's angry frown deepened.

'Well?'

She turned to Mrs Deering. 'Did he—did he give a name?'

'Yes, he did.' The housekeeper's mouth set in a disapproving line. 'He says he's Liam Thomas. And he's waiting to see you, Miss Latimer, in the small drawing-room.'

Isobel gave a little gasp of shock; she felt the blood drain from her face. Eliot was watching her closely, and he now stepped forward, turning deliberately so that his back shielded Isobel from Mrs Deering's view. 'You do know this man?'

'Yes. No—well, not exactly. I . . . I know who he is.' Isobel swallowed painfully. Eliot swore.

'And what the hell does he think he's doing here?'

Isobel raised her hand to touch his arm, and he withdrew sharply. 'Please, Eliot, it's all right. I know what he wants. I know why he wants to see me. It's . . . it's a private matter. I'm sorry he's turned up here— they must have given him the address at my stepfather's house—they had it, you know, because of Bobby. Please, Eliot . . . if I could just see him alone for a few minutes—it won't take long, I promise you—and then he'll go, and we can forget him.'

Eliot took a step back. He looked down into her upturned face, his eyes colder and harsher than she had ever seen them. He too was pale, and she did not doubt his anger. For a second she saw some struggle take place within him, and she feared for a moment that he was going to ignore her words and go into the house and confront the man himself. Then, suddenly, with a quick furious gesture, he turned on his heel.

'Very well. I'll leave you alone, then. But get rid of him, will you? Because if he's not out of here in ten minutes, I'll throw him out personally. Do you understand?'

With that he left her abruptly, pushing past her and up the steps. Mrs Deering moved to one side, and Isobel saw him stride across the hall and take the stairs two at a time. There was silence, then a door upstairs slammed.

Slowly Isobel mounted the steps. Mrs Deering turned to her, her face full of genuine concern. 'Oh, Miss Latimer—I'm so sorry. I hope I haven't caused any trouble. But Mr Thomas was so insistent, and I was at my wits' end, and when he said he knew you, that he'd driven down specially to see you—well, I didn't like to cause a scene.'

'That's all right, Mrs Deering.' Isobel pressed her arm gently, and moved past her into the hall. 'It's not your fault at all. I'll deal with it.'

Outside the door of the small drawing-room, she hesitated, her mind whirling. Then, getting a grip on herself she tilted her chin and opened the door.

The curtains were drawn. The lamps were on, and a fire was lit. In front of the fire, bending over a table and examining the objects on it, was a tall fair-haired young man—a man younger than she had expected, no more than about thirty-five. He was wearing tight blue jeans, a leather bomber jacket, and a blue shirt that Isobel instantly decided had been chosen specifically because it matched the keen blue of his eyes. He was smoking a cigarette. As she came in he straightened up, took a long drag on it, gave her a cool, insolently appraising glance, and then turned and tossed the butt end into the grate.

'Well, well.' He advanced a few paces, his hand outstretched. 'The little sister. Isobel, isn't it? We meet at last. I'm . . .'

'I know who you are.' Isobel came to a halt a few feet away from him, ignoring his outstretched hand. 'What I don't understand at all is why you're here.'

'You don't?' He grinned, and ostentatiously wiped his hand on his jeans. She felt his eyes rake her from head to foot, saw them linger expressively, taking in the coat she was still wearing. He raised his eyebrows theatrically, in mock astonishment.

'Not what I was expecting *at all*. Not the way Bobby described you to me, but then Bobby's an awful little liar as you probably know, and my guess is she's always been green with jealousy of you. Now I see why, of course.' He reached in his pocket for a packet of cigarettes, and lit one. 'I like the coat. Bobby rather made you out to be a Cinderella figure . . .' He turned and gestured, first at the coat, then at the room. 'Do I take it Cinders has met her prince?'

'You can mind your own business,' Isobel snapped at him furiously. 'This is not my house, as you rightly guess, and you had no right whatsoever to come here. I'd just like to know why you did, and then you can leave.'

'When I'm ready.' He smiled again, an awful insincere smile that lit his handsome, somewhat predatory face, but not his cold appraising eyes. With some elaboration he turned, and sat down in a chair before the fire, and crossed his legs—as if he had every intention of staying.

CHAPTER EIGHT

ISOBEL stared at him in horrified fascination. He was loathsome, she thought, loathsome—he made her skin creep. How could Bobby ever have got involved with a man like this one? She took a step forward, forcing herself to sound less antagonistic. 'Look—I can imagine why you came. You've come to—collect. Is that it?'

'Got it in one.' He smiled lazily, and gestured to the leather document case that, Isobel now saw, lay on the floor beside him. He yawned and stretched. 'I thought Bobby had been giving me the runaround a little too often, not easy to keep tracks on your sister, is it? She does get about these days. . . . However, I finally tracked her down in the West Indies—on the phone, of course. Bobby said she couldn't raise the divvies, and you were going to fix it for her. So I waited—nice of me, don't you think? Then I rang her again yesterday, and what do I find? She's had a message—all's well. Sister's come up trumps. So . . .' He spread his hands. 'I've come to make the exchange, that's all. Tried the Cotswolds, and when that didn't work, thought I'd bomb down here. Glad I came now. This is a lovely place. Really lovely.'

'Look,' Isobel cut across him desperately, 'I don't want to discuss this any more than we need to. The message was right. I have got the money, and . . .'

'Terrific.' He sprang to his feet, and reached for the document case. 'In notes, I hope? I mean, I don't want the Inland Revenue muscling in on it, do I? Now, you get the magic envelope, I'll give you this, and then I'll be off. OK?'

Isobel looked away. 'It's . . . it's not quite as simple as that,' she began desperately. 'I've arranged—a loan. I don't have it with me here.'

'Oh dear.' To her horror he sat down again. 'What do we do, then, wait?'

'No, of course not—you can't wait here. I told you— I've arranged a loan with my bank at home. It's all fixed. It's all right. I can meet you there Monday, and give you the money then, and . . .'

'Listen, darling, we're a week over the deadline I gave your sister already, and my patience is beginning to wear a little thin. You want the pictures, you pay up now. Otherwise it's back to London. These will be plastered all over the first edition Monday morning. I've got contacts, ready and waiting to go . . .'

'No, please, listen—don't do that.' Isobel stepped forward anxiously. 'I give you my word you'll have the money on Monday. In notes, any way you want it, truly—I've been promised it. It wasn't easy for me to get it, but . . .'

'It wasn't? You do surprise me. Looking the way you do.' He stood up, and to her horror took a step towards her. He reached up his hand, and before she could recoil, caught her arm, and began to stroke the fur she was wearing.

'Listen, darling,' he went on, his voice losing its banter and taking on a tone of more overt threat, 'don't spin me a line about a loan. You've got friends—rich friends. See that little snuffbox there—the one on the table, the one I was looking at when you came in? That's Fabergé, darling, the real McCoy. You could flog that for a hundred thousand, eighty certainly, no problem.' His face hardened suddenly, and the grip on her arm grew tighter. 'Listen, darling, don't stand there with a sodding fortune in fur on your back and bleat to me about loans and Monday. What do you take me for? Some kind of idiot? If you haven't got the readies, give me the coat. Then you can have the pictures and we'll call it quits. No more bother—OK?'

'I'm afraid that's not possible.'

The ice-cold voice came from directly behind her. A second later the door snapped shut. She heard Eliot advancing across the room.

There was a moment's silence. She saw only Liam
Thomas's reaction. His eyes widened. He released her
arm, and stepped back. He was at least a head shorter
than Eliot, and scrawnily built. Isobel saw a weaselly
unease creep into his eyes; the next second it was gone,
and he smiled. Clearly he intended to brazen it out.

Eliot came to a halt beside her, and Isobel glanced up
at him. His eyes blazed dark in his pale face; his arms
hung relaxed by his sides, but his fists were clenched.
Dear God, she thought desperately, when did he come
in, how much did he hear?

'I didn't hear all your conversation,' Eliot's voice
was coldly polite, 'but I heard enough. I take it some
form of blackmail is involved. Does that explain your
presence, unannounced, in my house?'

His tone made Isobel quail, but Liam Thomas was
made of sterner stuff. His eyes widened innocently.
'Blackmail? Blackmail? What a nasty word. Not the
word I'd have used at all. No, no, nothing like that.
Just . . .' He paused, and glanced at Isobel's white face.
'Just a business deal, that's all. She's buying, and I'm
selling. It's a long-standing business deal . . .'

There was a moment's stony silence, then Eliot
turned and moved to a side table. 'My apologies. I must
have quite misunderstood. In that case, I assume you'll
have no objections when I call the police. Just in case
it's not all as straightforward as you say . . .'

He picked up the telephone receiver as he spoke, and
started to dial. Isobel stared at Liam Thomas for a
second, and then spun round. 'No, Eliot, please,' she
cried wildly. 'Please—don't call the police. There's no
need, truly . . .'

Eliot's eyes met hers for a second, his eyes like black
ice. Then, very slowly, he replaced the receiver. His face
looked drawn, Isobel saw; lines of strain were etched
from nose to chin.

'I see.' His voice was quite flat and he turned back to
the photographer. 'Then since the deal is taking place in
my house, and the terms of it didn't sound entirely
agreeable to Miss Latimer, who is my guest, perhaps

you'd tell me ... what exactly are you selling and she buying?'

Isobel darted forward between them as she saw a smirk of malicious amusement light the photographer's face. 'Please, there's no need for this. If you'd just leave me alone with ... with Mr Thomas for a few minutes, I'm sure he and I can sort it out. I told you, it's a private matter and I'd rather ...'

'Photographs.' Liam Thomas cut across her pleading, his voice quite cool. His eyes flicked over Eliot's face appraisingly. There was a silence. 'Photographs,' he repeated, 'negatives, to be exact. I'm selling them, and she's buying them.'

Isobel crimsoned; she let her breath out in a shaky sigh. She saw Eliot's brow contract in an expression first of puzzlement, then of growing disbelief.

'Old photographs,' Liam went on imperturbably. 'Slightly indiscreet—shall we put it like that?' He paused, his gaze flicking across to Isobel. 'Photographs that I rather get the impression your guest would prefer you not to see. But then she doesn't want anyone to see them, which is why she's buying and I'm selling.' He shrugged, and took a step forward. 'However, if she wants to pull out of the deal, that's up to her. She won't object, then, I take it, when I sell them elsewhere ...'

There was a moment's silence. Isobel stared at the two men, even in her horror able to appreciate the quickness with which Liam Thomas had turned the situation to his advantage. She knew what Eliot thought now—it was transparent in his face, which was now etched in lines of cold distaste. He thought the photographs were of her.

'You have a deal already?' Eliot's voice stopped the other man in his tracks. 'May I ask the price? I presume you had fixed on one other than the coat.'

'Oh sure.' The photographer smiled. 'It was fixed weeks ago. Cheap at the price, really. Five rolls of film, two thousand pounds a roll. That makes ten thousand pounds.'

Slowly Eliot turned to look at Isobel. Not a muscle

moved in his face, but the stare he gave her was withering.

'I see.' He turned back to the photographer, reaching into an inner pocket as he did so. With polite formality, he drew out a cheque book and a fountain pen. 'In that case, I'll give you the money now . . .' He bent over the cheque-book and Isobel watched in paralysed horror. Liam Thomas did not move. With a quick gesture Eliot tore the cheque out, and handed it to him. The photographer looked down at the slip of paper, his face impassive. 'It's drawn on my account with my own bank.' Eliot's voice was cold. 'I assume that's acceptable?'

For the first time the photographer looked discomfited. Slowly he raised his head and looked from Isobel to Eliot, then gave a low whistle. 'It won't bounce, for sure—even I know enough to know that.' He hesitated. 'How do I know you won't cancel it, though? You could do it easily enough.'

'How do I know you don't have more photographs?' Eliot replied, his voice dangerously calm. 'For all I know you have other pictures and you'll attempt a similar deal. No, I'm afraid we'll just have to trust each other, won't we? Just so long as you understand that if you ever bother Miss Latimer again, or show your face again anywhere near her, I'll personally break your neck . . .'

'Hey—cool it, cool it!' Liam Thomas took a step backward. 'I'm not a fool. In the first place there aren't any more pictures—none I took anyhow—and if there were I wouldn't try it.' He attempted a facetious grin. 'Not with you around—I don't play the big league. I see why you were so anxious to get them, though.' He risked a wink at Isobel. 'Don't want any scandal upsetting the apple-cart now, I'm sure—not with a protector like this one. Hope I haven't queered your pitch, darling, I never meant to.'

'The photographs, please.' Eliot held out his hand impatiently, and Liam grinned. He lifted the document case, and slowly unzipped it. From inside he took out six thin sleeves of film.

'One, two, three . . .' He began laying them down on the table with insolent slowness, glancing up at Eliot as he did so. 'One and two aren't up to much if you're thinking of seeing what you've bought. It took a while for her to get warmed up—inexperienced, you know how it is. . . . But three's not bad, four's good, I can recommend that, and five and six, well, they're sensational.' To Isobel's horror he started to pull a sheaf of negatives out of the last sleeve, holding it up to the light for Eliot to see. 'I'd forgotten that one. Getting a bit carried away myself by that point—misting up the lens with the heavy breathing, and I'm a pro, so you can't see the face really.'

'Get out, and get out now.' Eliot took a step forward, his face white with anger. 'Get out, or so help me God, I'll . . .' He brought his hand down hard on the table.

He had no need to complete the sentence. The photographer was half-way to the door, he paused there for a second, as if trying to think of a suitable parting shot, and then, his nerve failing him, bolted. The door slammed shut behind him. They heard his footsteps hurrying across the marble paving of the hall, the slam of a car door, the frantic revving of an engine. It disappeared into the night, and there was silence.

Isobel was shaking from head to foot. Eliot had not moved. The sleeves of photographs were scattered on the floor. With a low cry, Isobel turned to him. 'Eliot, listen to me—it's not what you think . . . please.'

He turned his back on her with a gesture so furious she fell silent. Then methodically he bent and picked up the photographs one by one. It was impossible to do so without seeing what some of them depicted, and Isobel stared at them in mute horror. Then, desperately, as Eliot straightened up again, his face grim and purposeful, she found her voice.

'Eliot—they're not of me. I swear they're not of me.'

As she spoke, Eliot threw the whole bundle of negatives into the middle of the fire. At first their cellophane wrappers, and then the negatives themselves, flared up in a spurt of crackling flames. Isobel broke off.

Slowly Eliot turned. He drew in his breath; he was shaking with anger, and instinctively Isobel flinched away from him.

'Just don't *lie*,' he spat at her. 'Don't ever try to lie to me again, because from now on I'll never believe you—do you understand me? Never. You lied about that money—you've lied about your loss of memory—you were a liar five years ago, and you haven't changed.'

'Five years ago?' Isobel stared at him blankly, fear welling up inside her, confusion spinning in her brain. 'Five years ago? But you . . .'

He shook her violently. 'I've been through hell because of you—not once, so help me, but twice, because I'm such a goddamned fool, and you—with your beautiful sweet innocent face—you know how to dupe a man so well. Don't try to pretend you don't know what I mean. Don't try to pretend you can't remember . . .'

'Remember what?' Isobel gave a cry of anguish. Pain had started up in her head, throbbing, shooting from temple to temple; Eliot's face receded from her vision and blurred. Only his words got through to her, and past the pain in her head as he gripped her more tightly.

'You don't remember? Can't remember? *Won't* remember? Then I'll bloody well *make* you remember—and this time you'll *never* forget. Now—you're coming with me . . .'

He propelled her out of the room so fast, Isobel hardly knew what was happening. Then he half carried her up the stairs. He kicked open the door of her bedroom with a violent crash, and pushed her away from him. The door slammed behind them; Isobel gave a low choking cry and fell to her knees. The pain in her head was intense now, so strong she could hardly see. The familiar room tilted crazily, tipped on its axis; its walls seemed to rush in on her and then recede again into infinite space. Dimly she was conscious that Eliot was locking the door. Helplessly she raised her tear-stained face to his.

'Eliot, please . . . don't do this. I don't understand—you don't understand. Let me explain—please, if you'll just let me do that. You're—my head is hurting me . . .'

If he heard her pleas he ignored them. As the room righted itself and came into focus again, she saw him turn back to her.

'Now,' His voice had regained control again, though it was still icy with anger. 'Get up on the bed.'

'*What?*' She stared at him in disbelief.

He took a step forward, and Isobel backed away. Fear constricted her throat, fear and a horrible sick sense of misery. She hesitated, and then, as Eliot lifted his hand, something in her mind snapped. She backed away, feeling blindly for the edge of the bed, and then pulled herself on to it, crouching back on the covers against the curtains at its head.

'Not like that. You weren't like that. You were like *this* . . .'

In a second he was across the room, and beside her, pulling her forward so she was kneeling against him. His arms came around her then so tightly she could hardly breathe, and he forced her head back. Isobel shut her eyes.

'Look at me,' His voice was rough and desperate. As he spoke, he pulled her tighter against him, so she felt the sudden surge of his flesh, the instant of arousal, and she cried out in fear, and wrenched her head to one side.

'I said, look at me . . .' He turned her face back. Isobel opened her eyes. Dimly, through fear and tears, she saw his face, a face. Harsh planes, the mouth only a few inches from her own; it focused for a second, and then blurred in a spasm of pain so acute that she cried out.

'Now . . .' He drew in a deep breath, and she sensed that he was fighting to gain control of himself. 'Now—what do you say?'

'Say? Say?' She stared at him wildly, trying to free

herself from his grip. 'I don't know—what should I say?'

'You say—it's quite simple ...' His mouth curled. 'You say—*I love you. You must trust me.* That's all.'

'I won't—I don't ... Let me go ...'

His mouth came down on hers as she spoke, harshly and desperately. She caught the fleeting sweet remembered scent of his skin, and gave a low cry. Instinctively her lips parted; blood hammered in the blackness of her mind. For a second, what was left of her will and her rationality was there, making her body rigid and resistant, a great wall between them. And then it went, and she was sucked under. She clung to him in desperation. His tongue explored her lips; his hands moved up over her dress to cup her breasts. As the tension left her body, it left his also. His grip grew gentler, softer, he began to stroke her breasts and her throat, she heard his voice speak her name, felt his lips move on her skin as he did so. She lifted her arms and wound them about his neck, slipping back against the covers, and drawing his hard body down on top of her.

'Yes ... yes ...'

She heard his voice dimly, as if across a great space, and she arched herself against him, up to him, and he gave a low groan.

'*I love you and you must trust me* ...' The words were there, spoken, without conscious thought on her part, without effort at articulation, and she felt rather than saw him lift his head in a kind of sudden triumph. Then, gently and sweetly, he was parting her dress, drawing the hardening points of her breasts up to the caress of lips and tongue. She was shuddering as he shuddered, their bodies seeking one another through their clothes in a sudden desperation of passion that must be satiated quickly, quickly. Her hands were seeking for him, fumbling with his clothes, unfastening the leather belt, reaching for him, as he reached for her.

The pain was still there, but it was ebbing, and the sick sense of distress, of dislocation had gone. There was surety in his touch, in her touch, as she felt the warmth of his skin against her hands, the gentle pressure of his hands as he stroked her thighs and parted them.

'Lie back . . .'

She lay back; her eyes closed and she let the warm secret warmth flood up through her body as he touched her, gently, expertly. She felt his hands unfasten her stockings, and slip them off. Then his cool fingers were easing the lace of her panties, over her hips, over her thighs, and she was reaching for him again, as his weight came down on hers, reaching for him in an agony of want in which there was no time for more undressing, no time for delay.

'Now—oh now. Quickly . . .' Her own voice was low and broken. All she knew, as she touched him, and felt the power and thrust of his flesh, was that she wanted him in her, that that alone could bring release. She clung to him while he held himself hard and poised, and the waves of release beat through her body and brought tears to her eyes.

Then, and only then, did he begin to move, slowly at first, deeply within her, his mouth seeking first her breasts, then her mouth, his hands moving under her thighs to lift her body up to him. And then, as she felt the tide in her body turn, and start to build again, he was losing control too, had just enough left to hold back one last moment, his breathing was ragged. He lifted her up, cradled her to him, forced her face and her eyes up to his. Through the mounting heat in her blood, in that one last second before release for them both, she looked into his eyes. They were intent, concentrated, closed to all sense except this instant; they held hers for an instant, a second, no more, those implacable eyes she had dreamed of so long; those grey eyes filled with the knowledge of their joining. She cried out, and saw them harden in a second of triumph. His hands reached for her breasts; his mouth came down on hers; he moved, and like a star exploding deep within her, he took her over with him into the dark.

He moved quickly, and suddenly, taking her by

surprise, dragging her back from the deep place to
which he had taken her, where she did not know
whether she was awake or dreamed. He lifted his weight
from her body. He adjusted his own clothing. She
opened her eyes, the lids heavy as if she were drugged,
and looked up to see him rubbing his eyes wearily. He
was slipping a small leather case into his pocket, his
face closed and grim.

Very deliberately, he turned, and sitting beside her,
half lifted her from the pillows. He looked down at her,
at the damp tumbled hair that spilled over her
shoulders, a lock of which clung to the black fabric of
his jacket. She knew how she must look, her hair so, her
breasts pale and full, their points still hard from his
love-making, still uncovered, the dress torn. She felt her
mouth twist with pain; he should be looking at her with
love, her mind cried, yes, surely that was right, he
should, he must—and yet he was not.

His grip tightened around her shoulders; his hand
moved to cup her chin and force her face round to his
as she turned it away in misery. 'Now,' he said in a low
voice, 'now you can't lie. Tell me, damn you, tell me
you know who I am.' He shook her, once, twice, quite
gently.

Isobel looked up at him, Her lips felt swollen and
stiff. He had drawn blood with his kisses, and she could
taste the sweet iron taste in her mouth. His grip
tightened and she spoke, knowing the truth of what she
said, the pain gone from her mind at last.

'You're Julius,' she said.

'That's progress, at least.' He released her abruptly and
stood up, looking coldly down into her face. 'And?'

Slowly Isobel raised herself to a sitting position. She
took the folds of her dress, and drew them across her
breasts. 'Eliot Richard Julius Delahaye.' Her voice was
flat; even to her own ears it sounded dull and
automatic, like a child repeating a lesson learned by
rote.

'Better and better.' He gave a grim laugh. 'And?'

'And *nothing* . . .' She gave a low cry of despair. 'It's impossible. I must be going mad—you're dead. Julius is dead. He's been dead five years. And I loved him . . .'

'Liar!' His voice cut her like a whip, and she swung round to look at him. 'You're lying on both counts. I'm not dead—as I would have thought I'd just made fairly obvious. You never believed I was dead. And——' he turned away with an angry gesture, 'you certainly never loved me, then or now.'

There was silence. Isobel stared at his back, at the rigid line of neck and shoulders. Tears spilled over on to her cheeks. She could feel the pain starting up again in her head, black and insistent, swirling down and blotting out her thoughts. She gave a low muffled cry, and pressed her hand against her forehead. He turned round.

'All right, we'll try another tack . . . since you seem intent on continuing this farce. Though for what purpose I can't imagine—you can hardly hope to exonerate yourself now.' His mouth had set in a hard line. He moved back to the bed, and caught her wrist in an iron grip. 'Tell me your name—come on, tell me.'

Isobel pushed back the damp hair from her face, and stared up at him. 'I don't understand—Isobel Latimer . . . St Aubyn—what do you want me to say?'

'Neither of those, certainly, particularly not the latter.' His eyes flashed. There was a little silence, a beat of fresh pain in her mind. His hand moved down from her wrist to her left hand, and closed over it. He raised it so that it was between them, and as she gave a cry of pain and confusion, he swore.

'You are Isobel Delahaye, as you know quite well. The ring you're wearing now is your wedding ring, which you left behind when you walked out, and which I put on your finger a second time because—so help me—I half believed you, half believed your lies, and I thought then, if you had lost your memory—truly lost it—that it must come back *then*.' He broke off with a low, bitter laugh.

'Oh, of course, I had thought it would come back at

other times. When you saw me. When I kissed you. When I took you back to Morocco. When I made love to you on the same bed in which I took your virginity five years before—oh yes. I was foolish enough, stupid and blind enough, to believe all that—hope for all that, and suffer in silence when it didn't happen.' His eyes hardened. 'But then it *couldn't* happen, could it, Isobel? Because you hadn't lost your memory at all. You were acting all the time. Every hour, every minute. Damn you, when you were in my bed and in my arms and you cried out—you were lying *then*, and I could kill you for it. So . . .' He released her hand contemptuously and thrust it from him. 'Just tell me one thing, will you? After all, you've got nothing to lose—not now. Tell me—why did you lie? Because you were suddenly destitute and you knew I was rich? That occurred to me, of course. Or was it more basic than that—was it just revenge?'

He broke off, and turned away with a look of hatred so intense that Isobel's heart turned to stone. She bent her head, and touched the ring on her finger: two initials, intertwined. . . . She frowned, trying to force her mind to work, groping after the sense of his words, fighting off the pain. 'I loved you,' she said slowly, her voice halting over the words. 'I loved *him*. I think—I'm sure I loved him. You . . .' She gave a low sob. 'Oh please, believe me. I can't think, I don't know. I don't remember. My head hurts so much and . . .'

'Then I'll refresh your memory.' He turned back, his voice crisp. 'Help you along if that's what you want—if you're hell-bent on protracting this melodrama as long as you can.' He stood up and moved to a table on the far side of the room. 'Our marriage certificate,' he said. 'I got it out to show you this evening—tonight—before all this happened, because I still believed you, and I knew I couldn't go on pretending any longer.' He held the piece of paper up to the light. 'You married me on December the twenty-third five years ago, at the British Consulate in Morocco; my uncle arranged the ceremony. This is the only copy of the certificate left, I imagine. The others were destroyed—on my instructions.'

Isobel lifted her head and stared at him.

'We went on to the Palace Hotel, where we spent our honeymoon in the room you've just occupied for the second time.' He paused, and his eyes darkened. 'I thought—well, never mind what I thought. I'll tell you what I know. For me it was like light after dark. I was happier then than I had ever been in my life, or have been since. We chose that ring together—and the engraving inside it. It was our private bond.' He shrugged, his voice now desolate in its bitterness. 'In Latin Julius is spelt with an "I"; that coincidence amused us then. So we chose to have the ring engraved very simply: those two identical letters, joined together. It was a private thing—our thing. You were the only one to call me Julius, you see, although it was the name I preferred. All my family called me Eliot, after my uncle.' He smiled. 'You act very well, you know, I have to give you that. When I came into that room after your stepfather's funeral and you were introduced to me— nothing. You gave away nothing.'

He paused. 'I dropped the surname Delahaye after I came out of prison—had you known that? It made it easier, professionally, to escape from my somewhat unfortunate past, and yet the new name was close enough. . . . I knew when I met you again, and I intended to do that, you can be sure of it—that you'd recognise it at once, as no doubt you did.'

Isobel found her voice, and forced the words out. 'I swear to you, I *swear* I wasn't acting.'

'My dear, I'd like very much to believe you.' He moved back to the bed, his voice now lazy with sarcastic antagonism. 'Hence my behaviour these past weeks, which has no doubt given you much amusement. And, of course, I would have done, if that man hadn't turned up tonight.'

'I don't see what he has to do with it.' Isobel's voice faltered and broke off, as she saw his face harden, and he moved threateningly close to her side.

'Not much.' His lip curled. 'No more, no doubt, than all the others—whoever they were.' He shrugged. 'I could be flattered, I suppose. I assume I gave you a taste for making love. The only trouble was ...' He paused. 'I had to leave you, and you couldn't wait three weeks for me to get back. So there were the men your stepsister was gracious enough to tell me about, and there was that charming man tonight—presumably, judging from the glimpse I had of the pictures. And then, of course, there was Edmund. Tell me, Isobel,' his voice had become silky with threat, 'was it Edmund you wanted all along? Did you think about him when you were in my arms?'

With a low cry she recoiled from him. 'I don't understand what you're saying. I don't even remember your brother—nothing about him. That man tonight—I never met him before. Those pictures weren't of me, they ...'

'Yes, so you said before.' He laughed. 'Then do tell me—who was it in those photographs, being so inflammatory and so obliging?'

She turned her head away. 'It was Bobby,' she said in a low voice. 'I didn't want you to know—I promised her. She couldn't get the money he wanted—he was going to sell them to some newspaper. She made me promise I'd get it for her. *That's* why I came to you—to help Bobby. And then I went to the bank at home, I *told* you, and they promised to give it to me, and I told him that, but ...'

'Oh come on—I know half of this already.' His voice was curt. 'I fixed the loan for you—you must have guessed that, surely? I stood security. That bank's no more a charity than mine is, for God's sake. And Bobby may have her faults, but I'll say one thing for her, she's not a fool. She knew what you were, and she had the guts to tell me—and if I didn't believe her, I've only myself to blame.'

The room shifted before Isobel's gaze so sharply she thought she must faint. 'Please—tell me what you think happened. I can't bear it any more.'

'It's not difficult. There's a certain hideous simplicity to it—a symmetry even.' He turned his head away from hers, and she saw his face harden. 'We spent the week in Morocco. Your stepfather attempted to trace us, as we had known he would do, and failed. At the end of that week, we parted. You, my *wife*, still travelling on your old passport, returned to London. I stayed behind. The marriage had had numerous repercussions of a minor legal kind, partly concerning my inheritance from my uncle. We expected it would take no more than two or three days to sort them out, and that then I would fly back to England to join you. You, meanwhile . . .' His mouth tightened. 'You were to spend the time in London looking for a house for us, somewhere to live in together when I returned. You went back, and you stayed there with Bobby. Against my judgment—but you insisted. Bobby was your sister, Bobby loved you, Bobby could keep a secret—she'd never tell your stepfather. That was what you said, and you convinced me. It was all planned. Three days—four at the most. Then I would return, and we would go down and confront your stepfather together. And then . . .'

He paused. 'My uncle was involved in the car crash— as you very well know. I telegraphed you immediately. He was in hospital, dying: it was impossible for me to leave. I asked you to come back to Morocco—you'd always said you were very fond of my uncle, and like a fool I'd believed you.' He shrugged. 'As you know, you never came. You never answered the telegram. I telephoned Bobby's flat, and either no one was there or Bobby was, and you were out. She kept making excuses for you, and saying you'd been trying to ring me back, that you'd sent letters, that you weren't well— I was frantic with worry. It was impossible for me to leave—and eventually I realised she was lying on your behalf. Covering up for you. So——' His mouth twisted. 'Two and a half weeks had gone by—every second of them like hell.

'My uncle died. I stayed for the funeral, then I took the next plane back to London. I went to the flat and confronted Bobby, and she told me about the parties. The men. How she'd had to sleep with a pillow over her head because she couldn't stand the sound of you making love in the next room. . . . You weren't there, needless to say. By that time, you'd come back down here with Edmund, in pursuit of Edmund. Who knows? And so I told your sister she was a liar, and slammed out of that flat, and I came here. I got here . . .' He paused. 'I got here the day of the accident.'

'That day? Here?' Isobel stared at him mutely, and he gave a gesture of fury.

'Don't look at me like that—don't do it. That's how you looked that day. Sweetness and innocence, joy at my return. Tears. Some trumped-up story that you didn't understand why I'd been delayed, that you'd never received the telegram, that Bobby said I'd never called, that you'd come down here to wait for me. . . . I can't remember the details. It hardly concerned me then. All I knew was that I was with you again, the woman I loved more than life itself. And when I was with you I believed you—I thought everything Bobby had said was a vicious lie. You knelt up on that bed, and you held out your arms, and you said that you loved me—and I kissed you. And then neither of us could wait. We'd been parted two weeks—nearly three—in that time not a second had gone by without my wanting your body, wanting you in my arms—and so we made love, the way we did tonight. Quickly—desperately——' His voice broke, and he swung round to her.

'I know you must remember. I knew tonight when you did. I could see it in your eyes. You can't lie about a thing like that—you just can't. Dear God, there aren't many moments in this god-forsaken life when I believe in anything, but I believed you then. I believed in *us*. And you're so skilful that even tonight, just for a moment, I nearly believed in it again . . .'

'Julius . . .' Isobel's voice broke. She reached out to him frantically. The light in the room was growing stronger as he spoke; stronger and whiter and more intense, so it almost blinded her. 'Julius . . .'

He pushed her away from him violently. 'Don't touch me! Don't come near me. I never want to touch you again. Tonight was the last time ... what I want I can only get from you. What you want, any man can give you.'

As he pushed her she fell back against the pillows and he leaned over her, his face filled with a harsh anger.

'We made love,' he went on, his voice deliberate, each word like a knife in her heart. 'And you know what I believed? I believed I'd given you a child—I was certain of it. I thought it was impossible for two people to make love like that, to be *so*, and not create a child. I was certain of it. I laid my hand on your stomach, and I was *sure*. My child, our child—in your womb. I loved you so much then that ...' He broke off, his voice catching. 'That evening, just a few hours later, no more, I left you alone in the house. I had to go into the village to see my uncle's solicitor. I was away one hour, that's all, one hour, and when I got back, you'd gone. You'd left the wedding ring—just there, on the table. No note. Nothing.'

'I didn't take it off ...' Isobel spoke without thinking, the voice seeming to come from some dark recess in her mind. 'I didn't—Julius, please ...'

He ignored her words. 'You left the ring, and you left the house, and you went off with my brother in my car. Maybe you made love to him—I don't know. He told me you were lovers. He never gave me the details, and I wouldn't stoop to ask, and anyway, he was probably too drunk to remember. But whatever led up to it, you quarrelled, didn't you, and Edmund got violent—you liked his violence, he told me—that was why you preferred him to me, because his violence gave you a kick my loving couldn't do ... So you quarrelled, and you tried to get out of the car, and you fell. Then he panicked, smashed the car into a tree, staggered back here, and came to me.' He broke off. 'The rest is simple enough. I went to pieces. The rape charge was dropped, as you know, but the other charge stuck. I served that one year ...'

'But why? Why? It can't be true . . .'

'Because I didn't care, mainly.' His voice was flat.
'Because Edmund pleaded with me to get him off.
Because our mother was desperately ill, and if she'd
known the truth it would have killed her—she adored
Edmund, you see. Because it amused me—seeing how
easy it was to trick a so-called court of law. But mainly,
of course, because you made it easy for me.' He paused.
'After all, you told your stepfather I was driving the
car. You also told him a few other things. That I'd
forced you to make love, that I'd beaten you up, pushed
you out of the car at speed. It made a sensation when it
was read out in court.' He smiled. 'I had the marriage
certificate in my pocket at the time. It amused me,
that—knowing I could explode half the case just by
producing a little piece of paper. But I decided not to.
You obviously wanted to save Edmund's skin. I
assumed you loved him—and I knew how love felt. I
decided to let you have your way.'

'This isn't true! None of it is true. It wasn't like that.
I know it wasn't like that . . .' Isobel sat upright jerkily,
her face pale. 'He took the ring off. He hurt my hand.
He twisted my arm up behind my back, and he forced it
off, and—and he was fair-haired, not like you at all.
Very fair, and it made him laugh when he hurt me. He
liked it. He laughed and—oh God!' She bent her head
suddenly, and pressed her hands over her ears as the
pain shot through her brows. 'I can hear it now—the
way he laughed. He hit me, I think. He said Daddy sent
him, but I didn't believe him—Daddy wouldn't have
done that. He couldn't, and . . .' She broke off, her
breath coming in quick gasps, beads of sweat on her
brow. The image of the man before her came nearer
then receded into a blur.

'Julius?' She put out her hand blindly. 'Julius? Are
you there? You must believe me. It's not true, what you
say. It must be a lie. I never told my stepfather that—
never. You must be wrong. Please—he'll tell you . . .'

'Edward's dead.' His voice was still curt, but she
caught the sudden underlying note of alarm, and it gave

her hope. Her own pulse was beating in her head like a
drum, louder and louder. Quickly she pushed back the
tumbled bedclothes, and swung her legs to the floor.
She stood up unsteadily, swaying on her feet, her eyes
unnaturally bright.

'Then Edmund,' she said. 'I have to see Edmund.
He'll tell you—he must do. If I ask him—if I can see
Edmund he'll tell you the truth, he must.' She swayed
forward, and moving quickly, he caught her.

'You can't see Edmund.' His eyes met hers and they
were the eyes of her dreams, just as they had always
been. Grey, cold as ice, and filled with loathing.

'Why not? Why not? Why can't I see him?'

'I thought you must know. Didn't *Daddy* tell you? Or
Bobby? You didn't see it in the newspapers?' His mouth
twisted. 'Edmund's dead too, Isobel. He died of a
heroin overdose two years ago. I saw him often in the
months before he died, and he never changed his story.'

CHAPTER NINE

ISOBEL gave a cry of anguish. The room felt very hot, and yet her skin felt like ice; sweat stood in beads on her brow. She stared at the man in front of her, and his tall figure swam into focus and then out of it again. Julius—was it Julius? And these things he said, could they be true? They couldn't be—it wasn't possible, none of it was possible. It wasn't like that, she knew it wasn't like that, and . . .

'He's *dead*?' She heard the pitch of her own voice rise and then fall crazily, and again cried out in desperation. 'He can't be dead—he *can't*. It was Julius who died, not Edmund—you're lying to me—I can't bear it. He can't be dead. I have to see him . . .'

Dimly she saw Julius's face contract. The eyes flashed; the mouth tightened. He lifted his hand in a gesture of utter despair, and then turned away from her.

'If I had any hope left—any——' he began in a flat choked voice, 'then you've just killed it stone dead. I know now—it was true. All of it. One look at your face then . . .' He turned back to her for an instant, his voice slow and deliberate. 'When you told me you thought I was dead, that night at my flat in London—when I still didn't know whether to believe your preposterous story or not—I did observe one thing. One thing. That if you truly believed I was dead you'd come to terms with it pretty well. Not one shred of emotion in your beautiful face. Not a sign of remorse, nothing. But when you learn *Edmund's* dead——' He swore, and turned away from her once more. 'I know now, that's all. And I never want to see you again.'

There was a terrible long silence, broken only by the sound of Isobel's choked breathing. She stared across the shifting room at the rigid line of his back and shoulders. Then, with a low cry, she turned and ran to

the door. The key twisted in the lock; she flung it back
and ran out. The man behind her did not even turn his
head.

Isobel ran. Along the corridor, down the stairs, across
the marble paving of the hall. All she could think of
was that she had to get out of this house now, quickly;
get away from this man ... As she flung back the door,
and felt the cold night air sting her face, she thought she
heard a shout, perhaps her name being called, but she
did not stop or hesitate. The door slammed behind her,
and she stood looking out into the cold and the dark.

The wind had risen; dimly she saw the bare branches
of the trees lift and shift across the pale shape of the
rising moon. She saw them and did not see them. Her
eyes seemed incapable of looking outward; it was as if
they could only look in, look in to that dark swirling
cloudy place in her mind, where her heart hammered
like a drum—just one refrain: go, go, go *now* ...

She ran down the steps, almost falling as she missed
her footing, and slipped on the gravel of the drive. Her
breath sobbing in her throat, she ran to the car and
flung back its door. She had no plan, no thought; but
the keys were there in the ignition, where he must have
forgotten them when they arrived back that evening,
when that other car had been here ...

With a muffled sob she turned the key, fumbled for
the unfamiliar brake and gear, slammed it into reverse
so hard that the car shot back a few feet, spurting
gravel. Then it was in 'Drive', and her foot was on the
pedal, and she was moving, oh God, thank God, she
was moving away and moving fast. The window was
down, and she could feel the cold air rush against her
face, and all she knew was that she felt both terror and
release. She didn't want to leave, but she had to, she
had to. She spun the wheel hard, and the car circled
wildly, careering round, one wheel mounting a flower
bed. It stuck for a second in the wet earth, and she saw
a shaft of light suddenly cut across the drive as the front
door was opened, and she gave a moan of fear. Wildly

she pressed the pedal harder; the wheel spun, then held. The car shot forward, and she gripped the wheel. Light —she needed light—it was so black she couldn't see.

With one hand she fumbled crazily at the array of switches: the wipers came on and went off; the indicator lights flashed, then red warning lights, and then—oh God, the headlights—full on, so she was dazzled for a moment. They cut a pathway through the dark and down the drive, and she pressed her foot down hard and the car followed the lights. Gravel jittered and snapped again the car paint; a tree loomed up to her left and she desperately righted the wheel. And then she saw the gates in front of her and they were open, and she knew that if she drove straight out and straight on, it would be all right, she would be on the moor.

The pedal went down flat on the floor; the car surged forward, and the speed brought with it a wild crazy exhilaration, a lessening of pain. It was all right, she thought as the hedges swept past. It was all right, she was nearly there. She knew the way now. How stupid she had been! It was easy all the time and very close. If she could just get up on to the moor then she would be there, there in that dark space in her mind which had been closed to her, lost, for so long. *This way ...* She wrenched the wheel.

The road was narrower now, the incline sharper. There were trees ahead, and their branches met over the road and waved against the blue ice of the moon. For an instant her foot wavered on the pedal and the car's engine whirred, its body seemed to slow, to hang poised between space and time in the dark. And then in that moment, as the air rushed past her face, she felt her mind at last spin free. There it was, whole and complete, the whole sequence of events, all the turmoil, all the pain, clear and sharp and precise as crystal.

Stop. Stop the car.

She didn't know if she actually cried out, or if the voice was just in her mind, but she knew it was her own voice, and she heard its edge of desperation.

Stop the car! It isn't true. I don't believe you. He

*wouldn't—not with Bobby, not with anyone. You're
lying. Stop the car . . .*

But the car was going faster, cresting the rise,
careering towards the dark tunnel of trees. And there
were lights behind her, illuminating the sky so that
night was like day, and all she knew was that the pain
was so intense, and the fear was so intense, that she
didn't care any more. She just wanted to be in the dark.

Edmund, stop the car. She screamed the words, and
her hands wrenched at the wheel. She saw light and
dark, and the shape of a tree, and felt the frame of the
car lift and tilt.

Stop, she cried out, *stop*, and the noise of ripping
metal crashed in her ears like thunder, then the glass of
the windscreen burst into a million stars—beautiful
stars—such beautiful stars, she thought, for an instant
and an eternity. They lit for an instant and then died,
and she felt herself crumple into the welcoming peace of
the dark.

She didn't want to come back from that place, but
someone was making her. Someone was pushing her
and pulling at her, wildly and desperately, so they hurt
her, and she groaned, and they thanked God—she
thought they said that, he said that, this man who was
forcing her out of the car. There was no light;
everything was black, and there was a horrible acrid
smell, like burning.

'Isobel—Isobel—my darling. Help me—God, please
try to help me—quickly, there's petrol, it's all over the
road. Isobel—help me—try, oh God, please try . . .'

She turned her head then, slowly, and opened her
eyes and saw his face close to hers, saw his eyes.

'Julius . . .' she said. 'Julius?'

'My darling—yes, yes.' She saw something light
behind the desperation in his face, then he pulled at her
more strongly. Then he was lifting her, and she felt her
weight slump against his chest, against the hammer of
his heart. He ran with her then, ran with her in his arms
as if she were weightless, cradling her against his chest.

Then he was lifting her, tenderly, gently, up and into the back of another vehicle further down the road—a vehicle like a jeep, she thought distantly, with wide doors at the back, and sacking and straw—warm straw. She sank back, and he climbed in beside her, cradling her up into his arms, pressing his face against hers so that she felt his skin was wet with tears.

'My darling . . . my darling—I thought you were dead.' His voice was low and incoherent. 'Oh God, I thought you were dead—you were driving so fast—I couldn't catch up with you. My darling, my darling— are you all right?'

She felt his hands then, touching her body, gently and expertly: her face, her hair, and she knew she was all right, but that she had to tell him, had to break it to him, this terrible thing. 'Oh, Julius . . .' She clasped his face in her hands, and the tears rose to her eyes. 'Julius—I lost the baby . . .'

She heard his breath catch in his throat. She saw his face, close to hers, desperately pale, the eyes as dark as night, filled with concern, and then confusion.

'The baby?' His voice was very low; she felt his hands tighten for a second against her shoulders. 'What are you saying? Isobel—don't try to talk—you're in shock—you might be injured. Stay quiet now, wait, let me . . .'

'No, Julius, I have to tell you. I've wanted to tell you. Oh, I wanted you to know! When I cried, and you weren't there—Julius—listen to me—please listen . . .

'They told me you were dead.' Her own voice came to her ears from far away, and she felt the tears gather and spill, because she knew this really was not happening. It was a dream again, like all the other dreams, and when she woke up he would be gone. 'They told me when I came round. Daddy told me; they wouldn't let anyone else in—only Daddy. And he was so sure—and I couldn't understand. You must mean Edmund, I said, it can't be Julius. I love Julius. It was Edmund who was driving the car. He made me leave, he made me take off Julius's ring, and he made me get in the car. I hate Edmund—he's wicked. I never liked him, never. He wouldn't stop the car. He wouldn't let me out. I told him I'd jump, and he laughed at me, and drove faster. So it can't be Julius, it can't . . .'

She drew in her breath, and bent her head against his shoulder. 'I didn't believe him really, not ever. But I was so confused, Julius, and I felt so ill, and they gave me all these drugs for the pain, and they made me sleep . . . I slept so much, and I dreamed, and Daddy said it wasn't my fault, it was the accident, I couldn't tell any more whether I was awake or sleeping. And then . . . then I found I was going to have the baby. I was so happy then, because I didn't believe them, and I knew you'd come back one day, and I'd show you the baby, and . . .' She shut her eyes then and the tears spilled over on to his jacket. 'And then I lost it, Julius. They did all these tests, and I started to bleed, and they said they couldn't stop it, and then . . .' She lifted her head slowly, and looked into his eyes. 'When I woke up, my mind felt like ice. But not white—black, and frozen. I felt frozen all the time. I just wanted to sleep.' She paused, and gently touched his face. 'When I slept it was all right, do you see? You came back to me then, and you held me in your arms, and I told you everything, and you kissed me, and I knew you loved me. Oh Julius——' Her voice broke, and he clasped her tight against him. 'Oh Julius—don't go away this time. Please don't. I can't bear it if you do.'

'I shan't go away. I shall never go away.' He clasped her tight in his arms. 'I swear it,' he said, his voice breaking.

Isobel raised her head and stared at his face. It seemed so real, she thought. Oh, it was cruel—why did it always seem so real?

Behind her, suddenly, the road ignited. The crash of the explosion was huge, gigantic, like thunder in her ears. She cried out, pressing her hands against her head, and the night was lit with jagged radiance. Orange and blue; green and white. She stared at Julius's face, grim in the light of the flames, and as the sound of the explosion died away, she knew at last that it was true. No dream. No dream . . .

She gave a cry of joy, and saw the answering response in his eyes. 'The car . . .' she began incoherently, 'Julius, the car . . .'

Julius drew her close against him; he smiled.

'Let it burn, my darling. Let it burn.'

Isobel lay back against the pillows. The room was warm; a fire burned in the grate and outside the windows the light was fading. In a while Julius would come back upstairs, and be with her. She shut her eyes for a moment in happiness, and then opened them again, and looked around the room.

It was so strange. All those years of struggle, and now the memories came back to her easily, fluently, as if it were yesterday, not five years ago. This room: no wonder she had recognised this room.

It had been so horrible in London, she recalled, so lonely, and Bobby had seemed so kind and sympathetic. When Isobel had told her she and Julius were married, she had seemed angry at first, but that had passed.

'Married? He *married* you?' Her narrow plucked brows had risen, and the painted lips set in a hard line. Isobel had laughed happily.

'Is that so odd, Bobby? I told you—we love each other.'

'Darling, so you said—but *marriage*? I wouldn't have thought that Julius was the kind of man to . . .' She had broken off. 'I'm delighted, naturally. Congratulations. Well, who would have thought it? You do move fast, don't you?'

Each day, encouraged by Bobby, she went out and looked at houses, and each day, when she came back, pushing back the door, and staring at Bobby in mute enquiry, the response had been the same.

'Nothing, darling—I'm sorry. Now don't look sad, men are like that. They say they'll call, and then something else comes up, and they forget all about it. Don't *worry*. He loves you—you told me . . .' Her voice had tailed away; then she had smiled over-brightly. 'Try him again tonight, why don't you? The number's over there on the pad—I scribbled a message all over the bit of paper you wrote it on, and I nearly threw it away, but it's all right—I realised in time! Look, I've written it out again.'

Isobel sighed. How could she had been so naïve, so trusting, so stupid? But it had simply never occurred to her that Bobby, whom she loved, Bobby who was so anxious to help, who posted her letters to Julius, who waited in for calls—that Bobby would lie to her.

At the end of a week, after countless fruitless calls, she sent a telegram. What had happened to that, she wondered? Had Bobby telephoned later, and cancelled it? Certainly it had never reached Julius, so she must have done.

Eventually, when she was in despair, Bobby had come to her, her face full of warm sympathy, her manner contrite.

'Now, Isobel—you're not to be angry with me. I've done something that may make you cross, but it's for your own sake. I've told Edmund. Now don't get in a state—it's all right. I don't know why you dislike him so much, he's your brother-in-law now, for goodness' sake—and he's always liked *you*. He was thrilled when I told him—delighted—and he wants to help. He's come up with what I think is a very good suggestion. He says why don't you go down and stay at Julius's uncle's house—just till Julius get back? He says he knows that's what Julius would want. And you can't stay here cooped up with me in this minute flat, getting as nervous as a cat. After all, you know the house—you went there with Julius often, you told me. The housekeeper will be only too delighted to look after you. No one will say a word to Daddy until Julius gets back, just the way you wanted. And Edmund will help you track Julius down—in fact, he's sent a telegram off already. Now, Isobel, don't be awkward and fuss. It's much the best thing. Honestly—much as I love you, you're cramping my style a bit, you know. And you don't look well. You're pale, you're not eating. It will do you good, being back in that house. You've been under a lot of strain, you know, defying Daddy, rushing off like that, keeping everything a secret. Now go on—say "yes". You'll have to. Edmund's being kind. He genuinely wants to help. You can't offend him . . .'

And to begin with, the first few days, it *had* been better. To be back in this house, where Julius lived in his uncle's absence, the house where they had spent so many happy secret evenings together, where Julius had asked her to marry him, and—knowing how furiously her stepfather would oppose the match—they had planned their escape to Morocco—to be here, to be fussed over by Mrs Deering, to see Julius's belongings, Julius's books—all that had calmed her. It made her a little nervous, it was true, to know that her stepfather was less than twelve miles away, but since he knew nothing of her romance with Julius there was no real reason to fear. He knew she was safe; she had sent further postcards from London. When Julius returned they would face him together, and then the ordeal would be over . . .

Isobel sighed, and sat up. How incredibly foolish she had been! But she had been just nineteen years old, little more than a child, straight from boarding school, frightened of her stepfather and fearful of his terrible rages—so frightened that she had pleaded for a quick, secret marriage. And Julius had finally, reluctantly, agreed.

At first Edmund had been a help to her. She had never liked, nor trusted him before. Since the death of their father, Edmund had lived with his invalid mother in a small house some three miles away. Isobel had always thought him something of a mother's boy—spoilt and petulant, very resentful of Julius's intelligence and success, even more resentful of his closeness to their uncle. But this time she had found herself revising her opinion. Edmund called in to see her each day, never outstaying his welcome, invariably urbane and good-humoured, making light of her worries. Advising Isobel not to go out in case she were seen, he had volunteered to post her daily letters to Julius—none of which Julius ever received. Had Edmund read them himself, she wondered now, blushing a little—those outpourings of her nineteen-year old heart in which she begged Julius to return, or at least to contact her, and told him again and again how much she loved him?

And if he read them, did it make him hate her more? Maybe that was it. Certainly, the second week, his manner had changed. He began to drop hints, subtle ones at first, so subtle that Isobel failed to pick them up—then gradually the hints became heavier. Of course, everything was probably fine, just as he'd said, but it was *odd*—were they really married, she and Julius, or had she just said that to save face? Isobel had stared at him, astonished, and he had hastily apologised.

'Sorry! Sorry! No offence!' He tossed back the fair hair, and regarded her innocently with those wide blue eyes: Peter Pan eyes. 'It's just that . . .' He broke off.

'Just what?'

'Just—well, I may as well be honest. I'd have said Julius wasn't the marrying kind—well, we all did. It's a family joke. You know, he's very ambitious. We thought he'd wait till he was forty at least, and then marry a judge's daughter, someone who could further his career, not someone . . .' Again he paused, as if he had said too much, and Isobel had coloured to the roots of her hair, a sick sense of misery welling up through her. 'And well, you must know he's always played the field. You know how attractive he is to women—I never get a look in when Julius is around. I can't quite get used to calling him that, you know. Eliot suits him better: a hard name for a hard man.' He had laughed, a little uneasily, and then leaned forward, a worried look on his face. Oh, it had been well done— well acted, she saw that now.

'Isobel, what worries me is that I don't want you to be hurt. And it did cross my mind—you do know about him and Bobby, I take it?'

'I'm sorry?' She had stared at him blankly. The room suddenly seemed to pound with silence.

Edmund had turned away, as if embarrassed. 'Oh, well, there was probably nothing to it, you know—just one of his casual affairs—and then he met you, and obviously that was different. Except ... well, Bobby is very beautiful, isn't she? Still, that's old history. It just crossed my mind ...' His voice faded away. Isobel stared at him.

'What crossed your mind?'

'Well, I know you're very fond of her and all that— but I don't altogether trust your sister Bobby. I mean, the way she manoeuvred you out of her flat and got you down here ...'

'I thought that was your idea?'

'Mine? No. Whatever made you think that? Bobby suggested it.' He hesitated. 'And now Eliot's disappeared off the face of the earth ... you don't think, I mean, he couldn't be in London, could he? Seeing Bobby? Just to make sure she understands that it's all over—I don't mean to suggest anything else ... Oh, Isobel, don't cry, I didn't mean to upset you. Here ...'

And he had crossed to her then, and put his arm around her, and she had been so upset that she hadn't noticed at first how quickly his breath was coming, how the colour had risen in his cheeks. Then his arms had tightened around her, and he had brought his face down close to hers, and Isobel had jumped up and pulled away from him, and Edmund had laughed. And left.

Once he had gone, her face set, her hands shaking, Isobel had spent hours on the telephone. First she checked the number Bobby had written down, and found one digit was wrong. Her heart leaping, she had started calling again, the right number this time, the number of Julius's uncle's flat. When she got no answer there, she tried the hotel, the flat again, and then, in desperation, her nerves shot to pieces with repeated mis-connections, engaged lines, and bored and unhelpful operators, she had finally called the Consulate. After

being transferred through several secretaries she was
connected to one who was helpful: yes, she had booked
his flight, she said; Mr Delahaye had flown out that
morning. Yes, to London. Isobel had felt she was
dancing on air. She telephoned Bobby, all Edmund's
hints and suspicions forgotten, but Julius still hadn't
arrived.

'Tell him—oh tell him to get here quickly, Bobby,'
she said. 'Tell him I love him—will you?'

Then she had gone for a walk in the garden,
breathing in great breaths of the clean wintry air, lifting
her face to the sun. When she returned to the house, she
went up to her room, this room, and Edmund was
waiting there.

She had stopped in the doorway, astonished, staring
at him. Edmund was standing by the bed. In his hands
was the nightdress she had slipped under her pillow
that morning, a white filmy thing of lace that Julius
had given her. He looked up as she came in,
nonchalantly, as if he had every right to be there, and as
she stared at him, he lifted the nightdress slowly, and
buried his face in the folds of lace.

'It smells of your skin . . .' He pressed the lace against
his lips for an instant, and the colour flared in Isobel's
face; she stared at him, dumbfounded. He had smiled
then, a long, slow knowing smile that made sickness rise
from the pit of her stomach. 'Not what I would choose.
I'd like to see you in black. Thin black lace, with your
hair all loose over your shoulders, and . . .'

'Get out of here!' Isobel found her voice. She took a
nervous step forward, expecting him at any moment to
laugh, to pass the whole thing off as a joke. But he
hadn't. His face quite serious, he tossed the nightdress
back on the bed.

'I dream of you,' he said slowly, his voice slightly
thick, so she wondered for a moment if he had been
drinking. 'Day-dream of you. Dream of you in the
night. In my dreams you do all sorts of things—to me.
Tell me——' He took a step forward, and Isobel
recoiled instinctively. 'Tell me—is that what you do

with Eliot? What do you do, in your beautiful white
lace? Describe it to me, Isobel. Go on, I want to know.
After all these years, when I've thought of you,
dreamed of you, just the way our father did about your
mother—all that time, and then what happens? Eliot
gets in first, the way he always did.' He gave an odd,
nervous laugh. 'Still, I don't mind. I can share it, can't
I? If you just tell me what you do . . .'

She stared at him for a moment, her throat tight and
constricted, feeling first fear, and then, when he did not
move, an awful pity for him. She swallowed,

'Edmund—Julius is coming back. Today. He flew out
this morning, and he'll be here soon. Don't you think
you ought to go? You shouldn't be here—you shouldn't
be saying and thinking these things . . .'

She had spoken gently, as if to a child, and his blue
eyes instantly blazed in his face.

'Don't patronise me! You were always like that—
even when you were a kid.' He looked her up and
down, his eyes oddly vacant, his mouth slack.
'Sanctimonious little prig. Just like your mother. She
went after our father, just the way you went after
Julius—pretending all the while that she wasn't, of
course, that she was above such things. And you were
the same—little spoilsport. Do you remember the
games we used to play, Isobel—up in the attics—hide
and seek in the dark? I kissed you once and you
pretended to cry, but you weren't crying really, you
loved it. You wanted more. I'd have given it to you too,
I still would. Remember that, when you get bored with
Julius. Or he gets bored with you . . .'

Isobel turned away from him, shaking, and he pushed
past her to the door. She thought he was about to touch
her, to pull at her, to maul her, but he didn't. He just
stopped, and looked at her, and when she turned round
his face was white and pinched and miserable. She
thought she had never seen such self-hatred on anyone's
face; Edmund looked trapped, like a sick animal at bay.
The blue eyes flared.

'Will you tell him? Will you tell your precious Julius?'

She stared at him. It was impossible to tell from his tone whether he wanted her to tell his brother, wanted it passionately, or whether he feared it. Slowly she shook her head.

'No,' she said, thinking how much it would hurt Julius. 'No, I shan't tell him. Why should I?'

It was the wrong answer; she saw his mouth tighten, the eyes widen, as if she had insulted him. Then he had flung out of the room.

She sat up now, and touched the faded silk of the bed-hangings, then turned, and buried her face in the pillow. She had underestimated Edmund, and under-estimated the queer twisted strength of his feelings. To this day she still didn't understand who it was he had most wanted to hurt—herself or Julius. Probably Julius, she thought: Julius, the brother he both hated and loved with equal force, Julius whom he had envied since they were children together. He must have flung out of her room and gone straight to her stepfather—that was what Julius believed, and she thought he was right.

So, all the time she and Julius had been together that afternoon, when he had returned and they had made love, and all the lies they had both been told about each other had receded joyfully into insignificance—all that time, Edmund had been waiting.

And the moment Julius left the house, Edmund had returned. She still didn't want to think of the scene that had taken place then. Her stepfather had sent him, of course, and Edmund had enjoyed the task. Twisting her arm, forcing the ring from her finger, half dragging her down the stairs to the car, talking all the time, saying such horrible things, such filthy lying things . . .

She shut her eyes tight and thought of Edmund, her stepfather, and Bobby. Three egotists, none of them able to bear their own wishes being crossed. Three trouble-makers . . .

It was a crazy plan, getting Edmund to drag her away by force and take her back to her stepfather; if it hadn't been for the accident, it would never have worked. But her stepfather wouldn't have considered that, she knew.

In his rage he would have thought of only one thing: getting Isobel back under his own roof where he could punish her, where he would believe he could dominate her and break her, as he had done her mother. He had had a blind faith in the power of his own will—she saw that now. And even though he was dead, she felt a shudder of fear. To have gone to such lengths for years! To have told such lies. To have wrought such a chain of destruction was terrible: so many lives wrecked—her mother's, the Delahayes', her own ... And to have died as he lived, still sure he was right, still immovable, still full of hatred.

She felt pity for Edward St Aubyn now, not anger. He had failed in the end, after all. But then he had miscalculated. He had under-estimated Julius—the one man with a will as powerful as his own.

CHAPTER TEN

DOWNSTAIRS a door slammed. There were feet on the stairs; voices. Isobel tensed, and sat up. She knew who was coming; sure enough, a few moments later the door opened, and Julius came in, closely followed by Bobby.

There was a little silence. Bobby's perfume eddied across the room. She looked at Isobel for a moment, then shrugged her beautiful shoulders.

'Julius said you wouldn't want to see me. He said he'd promised you that he'd sort things out and then see me off the premises.' Her mouth twisted in an ironic smile. 'I said you weren't at death's door, and you weren't a coward. So here I am.' She hesitated. 'I didn't want to go without seeing you, curiously enough.'

Julius looked at Isobel across the room—a quick glance of enquiry. Slowly Isobel nodded.

'It's all right, Julius. Really. I feel fine . . .'

'It won't take long.' Bobby turned to Julius. 'I'd rather be alone with Isobel, if you don't mind.'

'I'm afraid I do.' Julius didn't even look at her. He moved purposefully to a chair across the room and sat down. 'I think you've caused enough trouble already, don't you? I have no intention of letting you cause any more.'

Bobby's mouth tightened. 'So protective! St George personified. How flattered you must be, Isobel.'

She hesitated then, but Julius crossed his legs and leaned back. It was clear he was immovable. Bobby frowned, then slowly drew out a chair, and sat down. She opened her bag, took out her cigarettes, lit one and inhaled deeply. Isobel looked at her steadily, and Bobby's colour rose under the heavy make-up.

'Don't look at me like that, for God's sake. If you're going to be reproachful and moral, I might as well go.'

'I haven't said anything,' Isobel replied mildly, and Bobby had the grace to laugh.

'Well, no, but I know what you're thinking. I always did. One of your failings, Isobel, you were always so transparently honest. You should watch it, you know.' She flicked a sideways glance at Julius. 'Men can find that sort of predictability a little boring, you know.'

Perhaps she had hoped to draw Julius with that remark; if so, she failed. His eyebrows rose slightly; the corners of his mouth twitched. He looked as if he certainly could not be bothered to answer that kind of jibe. Irritably, Bobby stubbed out her half-smoked cigarette.

'Well, I don't know why I came, really.' She shrugged. 'I wanted to make sure you were all right, naturally.' She paused. 'I wanted to thank you—and Julius—for sorting out that foul Liam Thomas the way you did.'

'And you wanted to check that we'd got all the photographs.' Isobel sighed tiredly. 'I can read you too, Bobby. Well, you don't need to worry, we did. As he's probably told you—Julius burnt them.'

Bobby's eyebrows rose a little, then she laughed. 'Good. That's a relief, anyway.' She stood up briskly. 'And you're OK? You look OK . . .'

Isobel nodded, and Bobby turned to the door. She was wearing a tight-fitting scarlet dress; black jet glittered at wrist and throat. She looked as she always did: spoilt, expensive, impossibly beautiful—a woman who had everything she could possibly want.

'Bobby . . .'

'Yes?' Bobby turned back, her head a little on one side, her eyes running over Isobel's face and hair.

'Why did you do it? Why did you lie?'

There was a little silence. The two women looked at each other. For a moment Isobel thought that Bobby was not going to answer, that she was just going to laugh and make for the door. But to her surprise, her stepsister hung back. She glanced at Julius, then back at

Isobel. She seemed to be thinking, considering. Then she smiled.

'I really can't bear you, Isobel,' she said gently, her manner perfectly matter-of-fact. 'I never could. Anyone but you would have realised that. Turning up out of the blue with your mother, wanting to be friends, trying to take me into your confidence, trying to worm your way into my affections the way you did Daddy's.' She paused. 'He was such an old fool. I think your mother bored him—except for a brief while when he thought he might lose her, of course. But *you* never bored him. You were always sweet and polite and affectionate and obedient. The perfect little daughter! Whereas I . . . well, I was just like him, and he hated that. He couldn't bear his will to be crossed, could he? And you never crossed it, until Julius . . .'

She turned back to Julius as she said that, and Isobel, looking at him, saw that his face had hardened. He had half-risen to his feet during Bobby's speech. Now, Isobel saw him hesitate; then, quietly making no comment, he sat down again. His silence seemed to infuriate Bobby all the more. Her eyes narrowed, and she turned back to Isobel.

'Well, that took me totally by surprise. Suddenly I realised that I'd under-estimated you, that you had a will of your own, a personality of your own—that you weren't the pretty, stupid little mouse I'd taken you for. It annoyed me rather, especially since Julius was involved. After all, he stood out, didn't he? The only man around here in this God-forsaken dump—the only man with any guts or style. And especially since he'd make it very clear to *me*—on several memorable occasions—that he liked a very different kind of woman.'

'I'd made it clear to you—on several *un*memorable occasions—that I wasn't interested.' Julius's voice cut across hers with a bored detachment. 'In spite of the energy and enthusiasm with which the goods were being offered. Why bother to lie? Isobel won't believe you.'

'Maybe not.' Bobby gave him a glittering smile. 'I

wouldn't be too sure if I were you, Julius. Isobel's awfully trusting, you know, and awfully gullible.' She swung round again. 'When you came back to London, Isobel—God, it was so easy—like taking sweets off a baby. It was just a game at first: I thought I'd just put the tiniest spoke in your wheel—well, I couldn't resist. You were so unbearably happy, so smug, so confident. And so bloody stupid.' She paused. *'I'll post the letters, Isobel. Here's the number to call. Why not go down and stay in Devon? Oh, Julius, it was terrible while you were away. I never realised Isobel was like that—all those men! I had to sleep with the pillow over my pretty little ears ...'* She mimicked her own disingenuous tones, and then laughed.

'It wouldn't have got me very far, of course. I realised that once Julius turned up. He isn't gullible, of course, but he is very jealous, isn't he? Oh, he slammed out of the flat and told me I was a liar, and I knew once he saw you again he'd forget what I said. A passionate reunion—I could see it coming. The best I hoped for was that just once or twice he might have the teeniest doubts—nothing too serious. Just enough to prevent your both being totally boringly content.' She paused. 'That would have been that. If it hadn't been for Edmund. If it hadn't been for dear Julius's marked masochism. Shielding your brother like that, Julius, honestly! I still can't think why you did it. I don't think Daddy could believe his luck, any more than I could. Really, it was all so simple and all so neat ... Do you know, Isobel, I used to say a little prayer every night? Don't let Isobel get her memory back—please God, don't ...'

'Right. That's enough.' Julius rose to his feet, his face dark with anger. Bobby turned to him, wide-eyed.

'Really, Julius? Why? It's the truth, isn't it—the truth you're so keen on? Why shouldn't Isobel know— she's been deluded long enough. We thought it was for her own good, Daddy and I, and as a matter of fact, I still think we were right. I even lied about what you looked like—she didn't know any better. She could have gone on thinking you were dead. You could have gone on hating her, and thinking she lied and betrayed you. It would have been much the best, then Isobel could have got together with some nice boring little man, and had a family of nice boring little children, and ... now, Julius, you're not goint to be aggressive, surely? And you would have finally shaken off your whole stupid obsession, and found someone else. Someone more your class . . .'

Julius had stepped forward and gripped her arm fiercely, but almost at once he let her go, s if it repelled him to touch her. He was looking at Bobby with horror, and Isobel, staring at her sister, felt horror too. Bobby's voice had changed as she spoke; she seemed to be enjoying her own malice. Her face had hardened and Isobel thought, *she's not beautiful, not when she talks like that. She looks ugly and old before her time, and ... and she looks exactly like her father*. Before Julius could move again, she slowly lifted her hand from the bed.

'Bobby, Bobby,' she said in a low voice, 'don't say those things. You don't mean them—you can't mean them. I . . . I lost our baby, you must have known that. That was what made me lose my memory. You can't have wanted that—you can't have been pleased by *that* . . .'

Bobby swung round. 'So what? Hundreds of women lose babies. There are too many in this world anyway. I had three abortions by the time I was twenty-one, so don't moan to me. I can't *have* children now. You can—or so the doctors said, so spare me the tears, Isobel. It's just one more reason why I don't want to see you again.' Her voice had risen as she spoke; its control had gone. When she broke off, Julius, without another word, moved to the door behind her and opened it with silent finality.

'OK, OK. I'm going . . .' Bobby moved to the doorway. Under the make-up her face was pale. Her eyes glittered, and Isobel was suddenly reminded of the way she had looked as a child, when she was in one of her frequent rages. In the doorway she turned once more, and looked at Isobel across the room. She had regained control; her voice was flat and detached.

'I can put up with all this,' she said. 'I can accept your being here, with all this money. I can even accept Julius playing the part of doting and protective husband. But the thought of you with children—his children—no, I don't think I can put up with that. So—goodbye, Isobel. Don't invite me to the christenings, will you?'

She went out. They both heard the sound of her high heels tapping angrily away down the corridor. Julius closed the door. He crossed the room, and gathered Isobel in his arms. Gently he raised her face to his.

'My darling. Are you all right?' He looked anxiously down into her eyes. 'I was going to stop her, and then, I thought, no. It was better that you heard her out . . .'

'I think so too.' Isobel looked at him steadily, then suddenly her face crumpled. 'She hates me, Julius. Hates me so much—why? *Why?*'

'My darling—look in the mirror. That would tell you.' He smiled gently. 'With all the money, all the skill, all the paint in the world, Bobby can never look like that. And she knows it. That's how it began, I imagine. And then, well . . .' He pressed his lips softly against her forehead. 'The rest is fairly obvious, I think.' Gently he tilted her face back up to his, looking down into her eyes.

'You loved her, you see. To a woman like Bobby, that's unforgivable. She despises love because she hates herself, and she thinks she's unworthy of it.' He paused. 'She made me very angry, and very contemptuous, and then—by the end—I just felt sorry for her. She'll end up like her father—you know that, don't you?'

Isobel nodded, and he looked down at her gravely.

'Do you want to cry? You should cry if you want to—here's the shoulder I promised you once, a long time ago.'

Isobel sighed, and rested her head against his chest. She loved him, then, for his gentleness, and his kindness, but she knew she didn't want to cry, not any more. She'd cried her last tears for Bobby. And her father.

The next day she felt much stronger; she was well enough to go downstairs in the afternoon. Julius wrapped her in the fur coat he had given her, and when he had finally assured himself that she didn't feel faint, that she did feel warm, he finally consented to take her for a short walk through the gardens. Isobel smiled at his protectiveness; he took her hand in his.

The day was warm. In the clear spring sunshine, the first bulbs were pushing their way up through the damp earth. Slowly, happily, they walked across the lawns that led down from the house. Down a path that bordered a stream, around the still flat water of the lake past the tennis court and down to a summer-house. As they passed each now familiar place, Isobel thought of the times they had been here before—those magical days before they left to be married. She knew Julius was thinking of them too; when they reached the lake he sighed and drew her closer to him, drawing her arm through his. In the little summer-house, sheltered from the breeze and warmed by the sun, they sat down and he put his arm around her. They sat like that, silently, for some while. Julius's face was thoughtful. Isobel saw his eyes travel across the water of the lake, up to the tennis-court.

'So many memories,' he said at last. 'We played tennis there together in the early evening, when the light was fading—do you remember? And one morning, very early, we went out on the lake in a rowing boat. And in here . . .'

'In here you first kissed me.' Isobel smiled. She raised her face shyly to his. His arm tightened around her at the memory, but he did not turn to her.

'In some ways that was the hardest part for me. I remembered everything, you see, so vividly. Every time we met, where we went, what we said. Even what you wore . . .' He paused. 'I even remembered the times we met when we were children. The times I thought of you in the years we didn't meet—after our families quarrelled. The time I met you again, when you were suddenly grown-up, and you were ... you were so beautiful. I ...'

'You were driving back from the station,' Isobel interjected quietly. 'I was out alone, taking the dog for a walk. My mother's old dog—do you remember?'

Julius smiled. 'A fluffy black and white thing—fifty-seven varieties, with a mind of his own. Oh yes, I remember. I stopped and offered you a lift. You said you were going up towards the moor, and I said I'd take you there, and ...'

'And we walked up there for hours. I remember. Just walking and talking while the dog chased rabbits, most of them imaginary. And then you drove me home, and you stopped at the end of the lane—I asked you to. I didn't dare be seen with you. And I felt——' She paused. 'Oh Julius—I felt so happy and so excited, so alive. And so frightened, because I couldn't believe you felt like that. I thought you'd just drive off and I shouldn't see you again. And then you turned to me and you said ... you said, "I want to see you again." Just like that. And my heart stopped beating, and I said, "I want to see you again too".' She paused. 'You see—I remember now.'

Julius gave a low sigh. His arms tightened around her, and he turned so he could look down into her face.

'My darling—oh, my darling. Do you see now—do you understand how hard it was for me? To remember all that, every detail, so exactly? To know how I felt then, to have believed—believed with all my heart and soul that you felt it too, and then ...' His voice broke, and she saw the pain dark in his eyes. 'And then to meet you again, after five years of hell, and to find you remembered nothing. *Nothing*. It was like a knife in my heart. I was sure you were lying. You had to be lying! I didn't know why—how you could bring yourself to do it. I kept thinking, telling myself, there has to be a reason for this. When she's with me, when we're alone in my apartment, she'll admit it then. She *has* to . . .' He broke off.

'And then you said nothing, there was no sign, no hint of recognition. When you used my name to me, and you told me I was dead, that I'd been a stranger . . . when I asked you if this man you were speaking of had a *wife*—and still nothing! I felt like a dead thing. And so . . . I kissed you. I had to kiss you. Dear God, I don't think I've ever wanted anything so much. And I was sure, certain, that then, then . . . you would kiss me back, the way you always did, and call me Julius, and . . .' He paused, and she saw his eyes grow dark with despair. 'And when you did not, I was so hurt, so pained—so angry. I said such terrible, unforgivable things because all I could think then was that I wanted to cause you pain too.' He stopped. 'My darling, do you understand? Do you forgive me?'

'Julius, I love you. Don't say that! How can you? There's nothing to forgive . . .' She turned to him passionately, clasping his hand tightly in hers as he bent his head. 'Don't you see, I *did* remember. Some part of my mind remembered. When you came back with my coat, when you said the same thing you'd said to me all those years before—I gave you the same answer. Without thinking, without knowing. Don't you see, Julius? It was there all the time—everything we'd been to each other, all the love we felt. It was there! Whole and entire, somewhere in my mind and my heart. And now . . . now it's there completely. I can see it again. Not just sense it, believe in it, dream of it, but *see* it.' She paused, and gently turned his face back to hers so she could look into his eyes. She still saw a little doubt there, and a residual pain, and she felt a sure calm happiness, a great sense of rightness and power because she knew now that she had the means to make that pain disappear.

'Julius . . . you know you believe me. You know I'm right. Look at me.' Her lips lifted a little. 'You see? The door has opened, the shutter's been thrown back, the veil has lifted—all those clichés. I remember, I *know*.'

She pressed his hand more tightly and went on, her voice low. 'We came in here. The honeysuckle was in flower. The light was fading. There was one swan on the lake—one swan, Julius, just as there was at the time I cried in that pub, and you offered me your shoulder to weep on. There was one swan, and we sat here, and watched him, not talking. And then you said—*I love you, Isobel*, just like that. No preamble. You didn't lead up to it in any way . . .'

'You mean I ought to have done?' His voice was dry, but she saw the light begin to come back into his eyes, and she laughed softly.

'No—you know that. It was right, exactly right. Everything was. You knew it and I knew it. And then . . .'

'And then I kissed you.' He straightened up, drawing her towards him. 'For a long time, as I remember. Not long enough, of course. And then . . .' His eyes grew intent. She saw his gaze fall to her lips and then back to her eyes. Gently he lifted his hand and smoothed one lock of hair back from her brow. He smiled. 'Perhaps one had better draw a veil over the things that happened after that. Certainly I was extremely impatient to be married to you, I know that. I wanted . . .'

'I know what you wanted, and I wanted it too.' Isobel stopped him firmly but gently. 'But you're running ahead. What happened *next* . . .'

'Yes?' He prompted. Her voice had grown faint.

'What happened next was that I said I loved *you*.' Her eyes widened in mock-indignation. 'You've forgotten that bit, maybe?'

'Oh no, my darling,' he said. 'Oh no, I haven't.'

And he bent his face to hers, and kissed her.

That evening they had an amiable and thoroughly enjoyable argument. Julius said that Isobel was still not strong enough to stay up and that she should have dinner on a tray in her room, that he would eat with her there, and then they would talk a little, and then she should sleep. Isobel said she felt perfectly well and perfectly strong, and she had no intention of playing the invalid any more, and that she would eat with him downstairs. In the end Julius gave in. They had been sparring lightly, happily, each enjoying teasing the other, and so it took Isobel by surprise when he suddenly turned and gathered her tight in his arms, and she saw the real anxiety and concern in his eyes.

'Julius . . .' she said, raising her hand to his cheek. 'You really are worried, aren't you? My darling, don't be. I promise you, I feel perfectly all right, and . . .'

'Oh, God.' He buried his face in her neck. 'I want that so much. My darling—I know it's stupid, but I want you safe and strong and well. I want . . .' His voice almost broke. 'I want to be able to hold you in my arms all night. To make love to you again. I want . . .' He hesitated, and then, drawing back from her a little, he gently rested his hand over her breast, then let it slip down until it rested over her stomach. 'I want you to have our child—to give you our child. I want to be able to hold you like this, and feel it move in your wonb, and . . .'

'Oh Julius,' she said, clasping him tight in her arms. 'I want that too. Soon—oh I feel sure of it. Soon.' She wanted him to make love to her then, wanted it passionately, and she could see in the darkness of his eyes how much he wanted it too. But he would not let her; he clasped her hands as she reached for him, and kissed her with such gentleness that she at last grew calm in his arms. Then he shook his head at her in mock reproof, and she criticised him for his control, and he replied that when he was certain she was strong again she would have the pleasure of seeing him lose it, but that meanwhile they should go down to dinner.

Mrs Deering had risen to the occasion. She had prepared a feast. With it they drank a bottle of that same burgundy—for old times' sake, Julius said wryly— that they had drunk the night Isobel went to his apartment. And then, when the meal was over and Mrs Deering had left them, they sat in the small drawing-

room before the fire, and watched some of the sticks of
sandalwood which Isobel had bought in Fez burn
slowly with a sweet fragrance.

Julius took her hand as they sat on cushions before
the fire, staring quietly into the flames. He smiled.

'Mrs Deering's very happy now.' He pulled a wry
face. 'It was very difficult for her, you know. She
finds lying difficult—and she was so fond of you, you
see. I had to explain, and plead and cajole to get her
to agree to all that deception. It took hours. She
couldn't believe that you could have forgotten, any
more than I could. And I was on tenterhooks, the
whole time we were here. I thought any moment
she'd make some mistake, some slip of the tongue.
And I also half hoped she would. You can't imagine,
my darling, how terrible it was, not being able to tell
you the truth. Wanting to tell you—every moment of
every day.'

'You nearly did tell me once, I think.' Isobel raised
her head to look at him. 'In Morocco, when you gave
me back my ring. I see now—you nearly did, didn't
you?'

'It certainly cost me a superhuman effort not to do
so.' His voice was dry. 'To have held the woman I loved
more than life itself in my arms, all night. To have
made love, and for it to have been the way it always
was, sweet beyond imagining——— True.' He broke off.
'Yes, I nearly told you then. I tried to tell you another
way. When I took your hand and ... do you
remember?'

Fire shot through her blood. 'Yes,' she said softly. 'I
remember.'

'Our bond,' he said, a little grimly, still looking into
the fire, and impulsively, pleadingly, Isobel suddenly
turned to him.

'Oh Julius,' she said, 'tell me properly what happened
to you. What you did—what you thought. I want to
know. I want you to tell me.' She paused. 'You see, you
said you hated me—hated the woman who had wrecked
your life. You said that if you met her again you would

set out to destroy her. Did you mean that? Did you feel that?'

There was a little silence. Julius stared into the flames. 'I persuaded myself that I did,' he said at last, his voice flat. 'I certainly hated your stepfather. I'd had five years to plan, and—well, let's just say I wouldn't have been averse to some revenge. When you've living without hope, and I lived like that for five years, revenge is a comforting emotion. Except that it eats you up, of course. It destroys you, as you sensed.'

'You meant to destroy my stepfather?'

'At one time, yes. If I could have ruined him, I would have rejoiced in it. He'd smashed up so many lives with his selfishness. Your mother's—my father's. They could have been happy, but your mother was afraid. As a result they did the right thing and everyone was miserable—except your stepfather. So . . .' He paused. 'So it wasn't an accident that my bank was so willing to extend credit to him, no. But after that I did very little, in fact. He was quite efficient at destroying himself. If he'd listened to his solicitor's advice in time, he could have extricated himself. He chose not to do so.'

'And then?'

'And then I meant to destroy you too, if I could. I made myself wait. When I knew your stepfather was dead, that he had left nothing, that I owned the house you were living in, everything, practically the clothes you stood up in . . .' He paused. 'It seemed possible then, pleasurable even. I intended to walk into that room after the funeral, and confront you with the lie you'd been living. You would recognise me at once, I thought. And then I would tell you. I looked forward to that moment very much. And then . . .' He paused, and looked up and met her eyes.

'And then I walked into that room, and you were there. My *wife*. And . . .' He turned away again with a gesture of resignation. 'And it wasn't as I had planned. There was one factor I had not allowed for, hadn't allowed myself to consider. When I came into that room, and looked at you, I knew.' He sighed, and she felt the tension in his hand relax. 'I loved you, you see. Just as I had always loved you. As strongly—more strongly—than ever. Just—that.'

He paused. 'So. I'd wasted five years. Five years of planning something I was utterly incapable of carrying out. It would have been easier to have cut off my hand than to have harmed you in any way. It was always like that. It will always be like that. And so . . .' He turned back to her. 'So, I tried, still, stupidly, to make myself hate you. I reminded myself of what you'd done. Of Edmund, and the things Bobby had said about you. Of the fact—as I thought—that you'd lied to your stepfather and to the police. I swore to myself that, this time, I shouldn't trust you . . . And I couldn't do it.' He lifted his hand to her face, and stroked her cheek. 'My darling. It was just impossible. I looked into your eyes, I touched you—and I was lost. Just as I'd always been.' Gently he pressed his lips against her forehead.

'I despise myself,' he said slowly. 'I despise and hate myself for what I thought and what I did. But that's the truth. Do you believe me?'

'I believe you.' Isobel took his hand, and pressed it against her lips. She bowed her head. The love which she felt for him lit in her heart. Not to excuse, not to plead on his own behalf, not to evade: that was Julius, and she loved him for it.

'You see, that night . . .' Julius gathered her into his arms, and held her close, resting his face against her hair. 'That night was like an appalling dream. I could never shake it off. I came back here—so happy. And you were gone. I looked for you—I wasn't alarmed to begin with. Then, when I couldn't find you anywhere, I began to be afraid. I went back to the bedroom and found the ring. No note, nothing. Just that. I couldn't believe it—I was almost paralysed. I just stood there staring at it, holding it in my hand, trying to work out what it meant—where you could have gone. Then I thought you must have gone to your stepfather's—that perhaps he'd found out where you were, had telephoned, I didn't know what to think. I rushed

outside, and the car was gone. Well, then I was certain
you must be there. You couldn't be anywhere else. I
was frantic ... I ran round to the garage to get another
car. I was going to come over there straight away. And
then Edmund turned up. He could hardly walk. He'd
smashed his face on the windscreen, he was covered in
blood. And he sort of slumped against the car—he was
in shock, I think, and he'd certainly been drinking.
Then he started talking about you and him ...' He
swore, and gripped her more tightly. 'I don't want to
talk about it. You can imagine the sort of thing. You
were lovers, he said. You'd only gone off with me to
make him jealous, and you'd quickly realised your
mistake. You'd come down here from London to be with
him, and you'd only made love to me that day because
I'd forced you to. That the moment I was out of the
house you telephoned him and begged him to come
round and take you away, and he did. That there had
been an accident...'

He broke off, and she could hear in his voice the
effort it cost him to go on.

'Isobel, I don't know *what* I thought then. I don't
know if I thought at all. I felt such sickness, such
pain—and such fear. Edmund said you'd been thrown
out of the car. That he didn't know if you'd been hurt
or not. I thought—dear God, I thought you must be
dead. And I left him there—just left. I drove like a
lunatic to the place where it happened. The ambulance
had already taken you away—no one could tell me
anything, whether you were alive—what had happened.
I went on to the hospital, and there——' He paused.
'There I met your stepfather. He said ... he said you
were alive, that you would live. But that you were
unconscious now—that I couldn't see you. He was
revelling in it even then, I could see it. He barred the
door with his arms, and then—then he said you
wouldn't want to see me anyway. That I was a bastard,
and he'd see me in prison for what I'd done to his
daughter. You'd told him, he said, before you lost
consciousness. That I'd raped you—beaten you up

because you'd realised the mistake you'd made in going off with me, and said you wanted to go home. "You were driving, you bastard," he said. "I know you were driving. Isobel told me. And I hoped you'd killed yourself. But since you haven't you can get the hell out . . .".'

She heard the anger in his voice then, and he drew in his breath deeply to steady himself.

'You know the rest,' he said at last. 'More or less. Edmund pleaded with me, he said I had to get him off. Couldn't I see that you were trying to shield him, and if I loved you the way I said I did, why couldn't I do what you wanted? He never wanted to see you again anyway—it was over, finished. He didn't want anything to do with a woman who could do this to his brother. But I had to help him. He had to be with our mother, she adored him. If any of this came out, she'd kill herself. It went on and on. And in the end—I said yes. It was easy, not heroic or masochistic, the way Bobby said. Just easy. I thought it was what you wanted, and if it was I didn't care what happened anyway. I might as well be dead . . . So I lied. Everyone else lied. I went into court—I, who had always had such naïve faith in justice—and a total travesty took place, almost without effort on my part. It was established that it was my car. Edmund and I had the same blood group—my blood was all over the seats, apparently. You had been snatched off to North Africa by me, against your better judgment, and in a jealous rage—when you wanted to go home—all this had happened. I pleaded guilty. I never even went into the witness box. The whole thing was over in under three days, and then I went to prison.'

'Oh, Julius! It's so horrible. So horrible.' Isobel clasped her arms more tightly about him, and they stayed like that a while, silently, the room still except for the flickering of the fire. At last Julius drew back a little, and looked down into her eyes. And, as she looked at him, Isobel saw that his face was no longer bitter or dark, but curiously calm.

'My darling,' he said gently, 'it didn't matter—prison didn't matter, don't you see? Bars and locks and regimes—they meant nothing to me then, nothing. The prison was inside my own head, the bars were around my heart. I thought you didn't love me—had never loved me, that everything that had happened between us was a lie. That was my sentence. That was my punishment. That was my hell.' He paused. 'And it's over now. It's gone. If I think of the past it makes me sad, of course. I pity you. I pity poor Edmund and the dregs of his life. But the important thing—the only thing—is that we are together and that I love you. It's the one good thing to come out of all this mess, and—in a way——' he laced his fingers in hers, 'I think it's a kind of miracle. Our miracle. That's all. Now all I want is to love you, and make you happy, and forget the past. I think—one way and another—we've earned a future, a long future. Don't you?'

Isobel did not answer him; she kissed him instead, knowing her answer would be in her lips. At last, reluctantly and gently, he drew back from her and took her hand.

'My darling. It's late. You should rest—and sleep.'

He started to lead her to the door, but Isobel hung back. He turned to her in enquiry and she raised her face to his, her face innocent, her eyes teasing.

'There's just one more thing . . .'

'Yes?'

'Well, I wanted to ask you before—and then so many things happened . . .' She paused and reached up her hand to touch his face, smiling. 'Your eyes. When you came to my stepfather's house and when I saw you in London. All the time we were in Morocco . . . Your eyes were different. Not grey, darker. I think if I had seen them as they are now, I would have recognised you at once. That my memory might have come back much sooner. So tell me, why were they different, Julius?'

He smiled; the stern grey eyes danced with mischief.

'It's very simple. I wear lenses. They're slightly shaded and they alter the colour of my eyes. I'd worn them for years—I never gave them a second thought until the night we were here and you told me about the dreams you had had. Then I thought it better to wait—and I did, until we returned here from Morocco. I thought . . .' His voice became dry. 'I thought, you see, that there were other parts of my body you might recognise eventually.'

'I see.' Isobel regarded him demurely. 'Well, I think I did when we were in Morocco. That's why it was suddenly so easy for me to dismiss the past, I think, because I knew you were with me. Julius was with me. He had come back. I think—somewhere, subconsciously, I knew that.'

'You did?' His tones were frankly disbelieving. 'Well, if you want the truth, I don't believe you at all. I think you'd forgotten Julius altogether, and you were quite happy with Eliot Richardson, the cold-hearted banker. I felt quite jealous of him once or twice. It made things difficult for me. Very difficult. I felt positively schizophrenic on a number of occasions. I remember quite clearly . . .'

'Nonsense,' Isobel murmured rebelliously, and Julius laughed, and swore softly.

'That's enough of that,' he said, trying to make his voice grim, his lips seeking the soft pulse in her throat, the warm touch of them making her pulse race, and her breath catch.

'Come upstairs,' he said, drawing her out into the hall. On the first landing he paused, and Isobel watched him teasingly as she saw him hesitate. 'I was just wondering,' he said at last. 'How much better you felt. Whether you—that is . . .'

Isobel laughed. 'I told you. I'm quite recovered.'

She knew then, that it would not take a great deal to tip the balance and those words were enough. His eyes darkened. His hand tightened around her waist. 'Good. Then we'll go up to my room.'

Very gently he led her forward a few steps, then, with a low groan, he stopped, and gathered her in his arms.

'I'd just like to make sure, quite sure,' he said, 'that

you know which man is making love to you tonight. Julius or Eliot. And if you make a mistake . . .'

He paused, his voice mockingly threatening, his eyes alight with laughter.

'Yes, Julius?'

'Then I'll just have to begin all over again.' He bent his lips to her mouth. 'Until you're quite—quite—certain.'

Harlequin Presents

Coming Next Month

Available in April wherever paperback books are sold, or through
Harlequin Reader Service:

In the U.S.
P.O. Box 1397
Buffalo, N.Y.
14240-1397

In Canada
P.O. Box 603
Fort Erie, Ontario
L2A 5X3

ATTRACTIVE, SPACE SAVING BOOK RACK

Display your most prized novels on this handsome and sturdy book rack. The hand-rubbed walnut finish will blend into your library decor with quiet elegance, providing a practical organizer for your favorite hard-or soft-covered books.

Only $9.95

Approximately 16" x 8" when assembled

Assembles in seconds!

To order, rush your name, address and zip code, along with a check or money order for $10.70* ($9.95 plus 75¢ postage and handling) payable to *Harlequin Reader Service*:

Harlequin Reader Service
Book Rack Offer
901 Fuhrmann Blvd.
P.O. Box 1325
Buffalo, NY 14269-1325

Offer not available in Canada.

BKR-1R

*New York residents add appropriate sales tax.

For the millions who can't read
Give the Gift of Literacy

One out of five adults in North America
cannot read or write well enough
to fill out a job application
or understand the directions on a bottle of medicine.

**You can change all this by joining the fight
against illiteracy.**

For more information write to:
Contact, Box 81826, Lincoln, Neb. 68501
In the United States, call toll free: 800-228-3225

**The only degree you need
is a degree of caring**

LIT—A—1